ENEMY I

Nick

A World War 3 Technothriller Action Event

Dedication:

This book is dedicated to my fiancé, Ebony.
-Nick.

About the Series:

The WW3 novels are a chillingly authentic collection of action-packed combat thrillers that envision a modern war where the world's superpowers battle on land, air and sea using today's military hardware.

Each title is a 50,000-word stand-alone adventure that forms part of an ever-expanding series, with six new titles published every year.

Facebook: https://www.facebook.com/NickRyanWW3
Website: https://www.worldwar3timeline.com

Other titles in the collection:

- 'Charge to Battle'
- 'Enemy in Sight'

The Invasion of Poland

The week after Russia's armies swarmed across the borders of Lithuania, Estonia and Latvia were the darkest days of World War III in Europe.

The brief fight was bloody and brutal. NATO troops stationed in the Baltic States were swept aside and crushed. Western governments faltered; stunned by the shocking venom of Russia's attacks.

In the days following the invasion, the Allied armies struggled to coordinate a response, giving Russia time to solidify its stranglehold on political and military power across the region.

Realizing the Baltics were lost, NATO command sought to defend the frontiers of Poland, marshalling forces from nearby nations and concentrating its defensive efforts on protecting Warsaw.

Russia released a vast column of tanks and mechanized infantry across the Lithuania-Poland border. One by one, the outlying towns and villages throughout the northeast of the country were crushed under the advancing army's might.

Allied troops streamed east from Germany, France and Britain to reinforce the American and Polish soldiers already in the capital. Russian artillery pounded the lush Polish farm fields into a bleak no-man's land of churned earth.

NATO knew Warsaw could never be adequately defended; the Allies were short of manpower and equipment; caught unprepared by Russia's lightning attack. To forestall the surge of enemy armor steamrolling towards the Polish capital, NATO command sacrificed small units of tanks and infantry to contest the enemy's advance – buying time to fortify the city's defenses with blood.

Drawn up across the roads to Warsaw, the advance elements of NATO's army were a cobbled together collection of tanks and infantry from fighting units around the continent who put their lives on the line so that others might survive.

They stared down the enemy and disputed every inch of ground. They fought with incredible bravery and ingenuity, knowing the future of western Europe might be measured by the minutes, the hours, and the days they bought with their stubborn heroism.

What kind of man stands in the way of an overwhelming army and defies them the road?

What kind of soldier fights on when defeat is inevitable?

NATO needed brave veterans; heroes who had endured combat before and who had stood defiant in the face of adversity and danger.

NATO needed men who knew all of war's evil and who would fight on until the end, despite the overwhelming odds…

Prologue:

Captain Oleg Khrennikov eased down the nose of his Su-25 ground attack aircraft and dived for the deck, skimming the contours of the gently undulating terrain with his teeth clenched and his grip white-knuckled on the control stick.

He flew southwest, following the serpentine course of the Narew River, constantly moving his head as he scanned the terrain that flashed past his cockpit to mark off each new steerpoint.

The river snaked through flat mangroves and past small settlements of houses. Clumps of forest and stretches of rich farmland blurred past in a patchwork quilt of greens and browns.

The mission's IP was the Zegrze Reservoir on the northern outskirts of Warsaw. He reached the marker and banked the Su-25 left, following the Kanal Zeranski, dashing over the two bridges at Nieporet. Past his right wingtip trees grew to the canal's edge in a dense corridor of woods, beyond which he saw the peaked orange roofs of residential suburbs. To his left the ribbon of trees bordered rural homes and neatly ploughed fields.

Time seemed to slow. Khrennikov could feel his heart racing. His breath came in short huffs of rising tension. Beyond the nose of his aircraft he saw the smoke-hazed skyline of the city and the Vistula River between high-rise buildings, shimmering like a silvered ribbon in the morning's light. He sat up in his seat, leaning against his shoulder straps. He pushed the throttles forward and lowered the jet's nose until he felt the trees along the riverbank close on either side of him.

Blocks of bleak low-rise apartments flickered past his left shoulder. The pilot peered forward to get a visual on his target. It was a multi-story industrial complex on the northern bank of the Vistula. Intelligence reports suggested the Allies were using the area as a forward command post. Captain Khrennikov narrowed his eyes, twitching the aircraft with a touch of rudder and stick to keep it on course.

Suddenly his cockpit filled with warning lights and urgent noise. His radar track and an array of launch alarms on the aircraft's RWR system blinked and wailed. A priority enemy radar signal showed fifty degrees to his left, indicated by a green inner light and a glowing yellow light.

The aircraft's RWR was a passive warning system; it listened to external radar sources then processed the signals, prioritized them, and displayed the results on a panel on the bottom right corner of the instrument panel.

Khrennikov tore his eyes away from the display and glanced sideways through the cockpit canopy. A dark shape trailing a long tail of white smoke skidded and snaked across the crisp morning sky towards him.

Instinctively Khrennikov turned the fighter away from the missile and sank lower to the ground until it felt like the belly of the bird was scraping the rooftops. The outer suburbs of the Polish capital were a maze of industrial buildings and narrow residential streets. At the same time, he fired off chaff and flares. A cloud of shredded silver foil exploded in the air behind the Su-25, followed by a stream of brilliant lights.

Khrennikov jinked right, flashing over brown tile rooftops, and put the missile on his six o'clock. Outrunning the deadly projectile was impossible, but if he could get beyond the signal of the ground-based radar system that was guiding the weapon, he still stood a chance of survival.

The clutter of the city saved him. Khrennikov zig-zagged left, then right, following a major road between a phalanx of high-rise buildings. His instinct was to wrench himself around in the pilot's seat to get a sight of the missile, but he knew that would be suicidal. Instead he sat in a cold sweat, counting down the interminable seconds until the threat display went blank and the missile lost contact.

Khrennikov breathed a sigh of relief and then one of sudden dismay as his mission target flashed past the right wing of his aircraft, a mile distant. He recognized the buildings from the grainy satellite photos in his briefing pack and gave a small groan of despair. His evasive maneuvers had thrown him off course.

He cursed under his breath, but not violently. To hell with the target. He was still alive. Now his duty was to find a way out of this hell-hole.

He glanced at his HUD. The steering cues on the display were chaotic. He flashed over a stretch of highway and banked to the right, gaining a little altitude and trying to relocate the broad expanse of the Zegrze Reservoir.

A clearing loomed ahead. It looked like a vast mud-churned field fringed by a palisade of trees along the northern bank of the Vistula. The field was filled with camouflaged military equipment. Khrennikov saw rows of trucks, and a line of American Abrams tanks parked by a small orchard. He smiled coldly and changed his weapons settings, selecting the racks of FAB-100 general purpose unguided bombs he carried beneath his wings. In his mind he juggled range and speed calculations. He glanced down at the ordnance selector by his right knee to confirm the correct weapons pylons had been activated and saw the corresponding green lights glow.

His cockpit threat receiver lit up again, warning that multiple search radars hunted him. In response, he slid down the sky, losing altitude until he was just fifty feet above the ground. He banked right, hanging the Su-25 on its wingtip, and lined the jet up with the clearing.

Buildings, vehicles, and a ribbon of grey road blurred beneath the aircraft. A wall of trees filled Khrennikov's cockpit view. He finessed the stick with subtle touches and went over the tree line like a thoroughbred at a fence, throttling to full military power and lifting the nose of the jet into a climb as he prepared to make his bombing run. He punched off more chaff as tiny insects of fear crawled across his nerves.

Khrennikov triggered the aircraft's CCRP targeting pipper on to the closest Abrams tank and glanced at the green range bar on the left side of his HUD display. He was two kilometers from target. His speed hit five hundred and twenty clicks, and he held it steady. Guidance information flashed onto the

HUD, and the pilot levelled his wings. The range bar on the display transformed into a countdown timer.

A furious flurry of tracer fire rose from the fringes of the clearing. Khrennikov could see running figures scatter in all directions. He heard the aircraft take several hits and the shrill screech of rending metal, but he ignored it. The Su-25's cockpit was an 'armored bathtub', enveloped in up to an inch of armor plating that wrapped around the cockpit and also protected the fuel tanks and redundant control schemes. He focused his attention on the line of parked Abrams. If he could not devastate the Allied command post, then destroying several American Abrams tanks would prove a worthy consolation. He flicked a glance at the readout on his HUD and willed the timer to begin counting down to the moment he could release his weapons.

He was at three hundred meters altitude. He aimed the jet's nose at his objective and held the Su-25 steady.

The rows of trucks parked around the muddy clearing disappeared beneath him. A jumble of numbers and symbols danced across his HUD display.

Khrennikov clenched his jaw tight. The seconds crawled by.

Three.

The tracer fire intensified until it seemed like he was flying through a hail storm. He could see soldiers on the ground hunched behind machine guns, swinging their weapons onto him. A green arrow began sliding down the timer bar on the HUD like a descending elevator.

Two.

The howl of the missile threat warnings throughout the cockpit reached a shrieking crescendo. From the corner of his eye he saw two winding columns of white smoke rise up from a clump of green forest to meet him. A dull alarm sounded in the cockpit to notify him that bomb release was imminent. Khrennikov felt cold sweat trickle down his face and soak his mask. He held the aircraft level while his instincts screamed at him to break off the attack and flee for his life.

One!

The HUD display indicators merged. Khrennikov heard a heavy mechanical clunk and then the aircraft seemed suddenly lighter. The eight bombs fell from the wing pylons.

The Russian pilot flashed over the clearing and jinked left, plunging back towards the earth as he overflew the northern outskirts of Warsaw. Behind him the city became hidden by a curtain of dust and smoke, lit from within by the violent orange fireballs of explosions.

Captain Oleg Khrennikov enjoyed a single moment of grim satisfaction for a task successfully accomplished – before two SAM missiles burst through the veil of dust on thin feathers of flame. They bore in relentlessly on the hapless Russian fighter and Khrennikov could only watch with fatalistic dismay. Both missiles struck the aircraft and blew the Su-25 apart.

The savage impact wrenched the right wing from the fuselage and sent the wreckage cartwheeling across the sky in a maelstrom of black smoke and flames. The twisted debris plunged to the ground, then erupted in a pyre of black oily smoke.

WARSAW
POLAND

Chapter 1:

The soldier stepped to the side of the road and dropped the tattered assault pack containing his belongings at his feet. It had rained during the night. The blacktop was slick, the pre-dawn light soft and misted. Arc lights from the military base cut stark elongated shadows through the high security fencing.

He was a tall, well-built man in his mid-forties, hair greying at the temples, shoulders solid with muscle under his uniform, and radiated about him that indefinable quality that only a veteran soldier gives off; a mixture of assured confidence and composure that was apparent in the way he held himself.

After a few minutes an Army truck arrived at the base and braked to a stop at the security gates. The man watched the moment with idle interest, his mind elsewhere, picking at stray thoughts. He reached into his pocket for a cigarette to while away the time.

Across the skyline the grey glow of new morning was struck by the flicker of distant gunfire, and the fury of the barrage rumbled across the clouds.

The man lit his cigarette and noticed a shadow moving on the far side of the road. A moment later a young boy dashed across the blacktop, splashing through puddles. He looked about eight years old; a starved grubby urchin shivering in the cold, dressed in a scruffy school uniform.

"Hey, Yankee soldier," the boy's words were thickly accented. He smiled with impish guile. "Do you want to buy a camera?" The child reached beneath his threadbare sweater and produced an old Nikon.

The soldier arched his eyebrows, bemused. He studied the child carefully under the flare of the base lights. The boy was rail-thin; his face very pale. His eyes were set deep into their sockets, giving him a haunted, weary countenance.

"Where do you live?" The man took the camera and turned it over in his hands. The lens had a crack, and a couple of the buttons were missing. It was useless.

The boy pointed into the distance. "About a mile down the road."

"When did you last eat?" The man asked gently.

"Yesterday."

The soldier crushed the cigarette under the heel of his boot and made a contemplative face. He looked at the camera again, frowning.

"How much?"

"Five dollars," the boy cupped his hands in a beggar's gesture.

The man regarded the child carefully. "What will you do with the money?"

"Give it to my mother," the boy's voice turned solemn. "My father is away fighting the Russians and there is me and my three younger sisters to feed."

The man grunted. He reached into his pocket and held out a twenty-dollar bill. "This is all I have," he said handing the money over. The boy's eyes seemed to expand into luminous pools of wonder. "Give it to your mom."

The boy snatched up the money and started to run, his expression one of desperate fright lest the prize be taken from him. A shout cut through the dawn.

"Halt! Stay where you are."

One of the base sentries, his weapon raised, came splashing along the muddy roadside verge. His eyes were fixed on the Polish child. "I warned you yesterday, boy. You're not allowed near the perimeter of the base. If you come back again, I'm gonna shoot you."

The child scampered into the shadows. The sentry gave an apologetic shrug. "Sorry, sir. Was the kid bothering you?"

"No."

"Can I ask why you're standing outside the base, sir?"

"I'm waiting."

"Waiting for what?"

"I'm waiting to go back to war," the soldier said.

The sentry noticed the combat patch on the other man's right sleeve and his expression changed to one of respect. He took a step back and lowered his weapon. A set of slitted headlights loomed out of the gloom, speeding down the road and throwing up a rooster-tail of misted spray in its wake. The vehicle braked to a halt and an officer leaned through the passenger side window of the Humvee.

"I'm looking for Lieutenant Travis Wayland?"

The soldier picked up his assault pack, hefted it onto his shoulder, and gave the officer in the Humvee a long level stare with eyes that were steel blue and steady. "You found me."

*

The private driving the Humvee turned off the highway, and as soon as it hit the side road, dark mud sprayed out from beneath its back wheels. It was the CO's vehicle and carried no weapons – one of the older models attached to the tank company's headquarters.

The private drove with his foot crushing the gas pedal against the floorboards. A chill wind blasted through gaps in the doors. He drove hunched over the steering wheel, the windshield wipers a blur as the vehicle raced towards the pale watery sunrise.

The only sounds in the cabin was the rattle of the vehicle's body panels and the roar of the engine.

Sitting up front beside the driver, First Lieutenant Huck Grimmet twisted round until he was looking at Wayland slumped sideways in the back seat.

"I read through your record. Impressive," Lieutenant Grimmet said as the Humvee turned at an intersection. He was the tank company's Executive Officer. "You served in Desert Storm with the 2nd Armored Cavalry regiment."

"That's right," Wayland said.

"Did you see action during the Battle of the 73rd Easting?"

"Yeah, but not enough to ever make it into anyone's memoirs."

Grimmet smiled. "And then you served in OIF, right?"

"Yes," the conversation, Wayland decided, seemed more like an interview. "I was part of Operation Iraqi Freedom with the 1st Cavalry Division."

"How long were you in country?"

"Fifteen months."

"You've had a long career…"

"I joined up in August '89 and served until '92. I took a break in service after that and rejoined in September 2001," Wayland encapsulated over twenty years of his life in a single, featureless sentence.

"After 9/11?"

"Yeah."

"How long were you an SFC?"

"Six years – right up until two weeks ago…"

"… When suddenly you were awarded a battlefield commission and promoted in the field to 2nd Lieutenant."

"Yes."

Huck Grimmet shook his head in admiration. "I gotta say, from the little I heard and the brief report in your file, that was some hardcore Rambo shit you pulled."

Wayland said nothing. Ahead of them an old truck pulled onto the road, belching a cloud of black diesel. The private stomped hard on the Humvee's brakes and cursed under his breath.

For several minutes the conversation inside the vehicle stalled until the truck swerved onto the shoulder of the road and the Humvee leaped forward like a scalded beast, dashing over the crest of a rise so quickly that for a moment Wayland swore they became airborne.

"What happened that morning?" Lieutenant Grimmet asked. "The day you won your battlefield promotion? The details in your file are sketchy…"

Wayland grunted and stared out through a window. The countryside was a broad expanse of gentle rolling hills, much of it furrowed with newly-planted crops, separated by stands of tall green trees. "It was at a place called Jekabpils in Lithuania."

"What happened?"

"I can barely remember the details," Wayland confessed, even though the battle had occurred just a couple of weeks earlier. "I was with a unit of Abrams tanks on exercises when the war broke out. We heard the Russians were pouring across the border, so we fell back on Jekabpils and joined up with 'C' Squadron of the Royal Canadian Dragoons. They had a couple of dozen Leopard tanks and there were some Latvian mechanized infantry already in the town preparing defenses. It wasn't much compared to what the Russians were about to throw against us."

"But you defended the town?"

"We fought the Russians to a standstill for a couple of days but then they broke through on the left flank and the whole line was threatened. The battalion commander's Humvee was hit by a stray Russian mortar shell while his headquarters section was withdrawing. The vehicle rolled over on the side of the road and a couple of aides were injured."

For a long moment his voice trailed off and Grimmet began to wonder whether Wayland would finish his retelling of the event. Wayland drew a deep breath like he was waking from a dream. He smiled; an expression without humor, and went on, his voice scrubbed of all emotion.

"The Russians closed in. A couple of T-72s and a handful of old BMP-2s carrying mechanized infantry appeared through a screen of trees two hundred yards away."

"Where were you?"

"Trying to get the hell down the road, as far away as possible," Wayland admitted. "We were in full retreat. The Russians were pressing us hard. The Canadians had taken a beating and so had we. We lost six Abrams in the fight. All I was trying to do was get my tank and my crew to safety."

"So how did you win your commission?"

"Suicidal stupidity," Wayland said. "I saw the Russians closing and I swung my tank across the road, putting myself between the crashed Humvee and the enemy. Then we opened fire."

"And…?"

"And we knocked out both the tanks and three of the BMPs. The last three enemy vehicles turned and disappeared behind a ridge, covering their retreat with smoke."

"You saved the Lieutenant Colonel's life." It was a statement, not a question.

"I and my crew held the enemy off long enough for the Lieutenant Colonel and his support staff to be rescued by another Humvee," Wayland qualified.

"And you got a Silver Star."

"So I was told."

"You don't care?"

"Not much. I never was one for medals."

Huck Grimmet sat silent for a long reflective moment. He had never seen combat, never commanded his tank against an enemy capable of fighting back. Next to Travis Wayland the XO felt like a fraud. He shot the other man a furtive glance, judging whether he should continue speaking. The private turned the Humvee onto a muddy track that slashed through a field of lettuce. The vehicle bucked over the uneven terrain, jouncing the men in their seats. Morning had come to Poland, bleak and grey, the sky overhead leaden with clouds the color of old bruises.

"I have to warn you, Wayland," Lieutenant Grimmet sounded suddenly discomfited, "there's a good chance that Captain Kohn isn't going to be too pleased to have you commanding one of his platoons."

"Is that so, sir?"

"Yeah," Grimmet nodded. "I think the Captain is intimidated by you – by your service record, I mean. He complained holy hell to Battalion when he heard you were replacing Lieutenant Smith. But the old man was insistent.

Kohn feels like he is being stuck with you and he ain't too happy about it."

"He doesn't think a man given a battlefield commission is a proper officer?"

"Oh, nothing like that!" the Lieutenant smiled. "He's just shit-scared you're going to show him up in combat," the Company XO admitted in a moment of candid honesty.

Wayland said nothing.

The muddy track wound around a stand of trees and followed the meandering course of a stream for a couple of miles before climbing a gentle rise. Wayland could see an old two-story stone farmhouse in the distance with a sagging porch and a couple of wind-swept wooden barns nearby.

"You'll be leading 1st Platoon, 'Cold Steel' Company. They're bivouacked at that farmhouse up ahead," Grimmet pointed through the mud-spattered windshield. "Everyone in the platoon is still pretty shaken up over the death of Lieutenant Smith. He was popular. He was killed two days ago on the outskirts of Warsaw, caught in a bombing raid by a Russian Su-25. The men took the news pretty badly."

Wayland said nothing. Behind a hedge of bushes close to the farmhouse he could see the turret of an Abrams tank, and the shadowed outline of another in the open door of a barn.

The driver set the Humvee to the crest. Lieutenant Grimmet's voice became brisk and business-like.

"The battlefront is very fluid. There is a lot of chaos and confusion. The control system between allied forces has so far been diabolical. Different command structures, different languages, different communication protocols. A lot of that stuff is still being sorted out," Grimmet gave Wayland a rundown of the bleak situation across northern Poland. "NATO is discovering that communication procedures that worked during an exercise don't work as smoothly when bullets are flying. We've been on the back foot since this war started, and we still aren't up to speed. But I can tell you we're expecting action any day. The Russians are closing on Warsaw. Sooner or later there's going to be a battle."

The driver pulled the Humvee onto the verge of the track and switched off the engine. Lieutenant Grimmet thrust out his hand. "Welcome to 'Cold Steel'."

"Thanks." Wayland kicked open the rear door and tossed his assault pack out onto the muddy grass. Lieutenant Grimmet leaned through the passenger side window.

"Captain Kohn will call around and meet with you later in the morning. He's at Battalion for a briefing. He'll have orders when he arrives… do you want me to introduce you to the platoon?"

"No," Wayland shook his head. "I'll handle the introductions."

*

Wayland left his assault pack on the porch and walked a slow circuit of the farmhouse. The building was eerily silent, cast in long cold shadows. Overhead storm clouds rolled in on a chill wind, spreading across the skyline and dropping close to the earth, heavy with the rain they carried. Against the belly of the clouds that crouched low upon the eastern horizon, Wayland could see a faint orange glow of reflected flickering light that faded and grew stronger, then faded and grew again. It was the light of artillery fire beneath a dark scar of smoke. The sound of the barrage was muted by the clouds and distance so that the noise of it was like the rumble of a far away truck.

He stood in the shadows and turned a slow circle. The farmhouse sat on a low-level rise, surrounded on every side by a quilt of green and brown fields, separated by hedgerows and a network of narrow muddy tracks. To the west hunched the cluttered outskirts of Warsaw, misted behind a passing rain shower. To the south cut the main road that ran towards the Lithuanian border; a straight grey line in the landscape, partially obscured by clumps of trees and a smatter of other farms.

Wayland walked to the rear of the farmhouse. There were two M1A2 Abrams tanks parked beneath draped curtains of camouflage netting. The tanks were grey with dust, covered in spatters of mud and grime, their tracks choked with churned grass. One of the vehicles was missing a right-side panel of sideskirt armor. He found another of the platoon tanks inside the open doors of a barn. He climbed up onto the hull and ran his eyes over the tank. The top of the turret was covered in bird droppings from pigeons roosting in the rafters, and the bustle racks used to stow crew equipment and supplies were empty.

The final M1A2 in the four-tank platoon stood seemingly forlorn and neglected on the far side of the farmhouse beneath the spreading branches of a tree. A stray cat lay curled up on one of the mudguards and the hull was buried under a drift of fallen leaves. The tank's armor was pitted with a dozen bright silver indentations that might have been the result of shrapnel fragments.

Wayland went up the steps of the porch with his hands balled into fists, his features a dark scowl of temper. He kicked the front door in and stood in the threshold. The door splintered back against its hinges and a shaft of light spilled across the interior.

The front room of the farmhouse was thick with the stench of cigarette smoke and sweaty unwashed bodies. Wayland could see lumpen figures laying on the floor and slumped in sofa chairs. An empty bottle and a dozen crumpled beer cans littered the stained carpet beside a brimming ashtray. Someone in the gloom groaned. Wayland picked up a wooden chair and flung it through the nearest window. The glass exploded outwards and the sound in the small confined space crashed like a gunshot. Cold air and daylight washed through the room. A man lying face-down on a sofa suddenly jerked upright and blinked in owlish confusion.

"What the fuck…?"

"Get up!" Wayland shouted in his booming Sergeant's growl; a voice honed across windswept parade grounds and battlefields throughout the Middle East for years. "Everybody up, right now!"

He went around the room, kicking legs and shouting in sleeping men's faces. The soldiers came awake, groggy and unsteady, their eyes bloodshot, their faces sallow and unshaven. Wayland stormed down a corridor and kicked open the next closed door with a single lusty crack of his boot. It was a bedroom. There were men asleep on the floor, and two naked women asleep in a tangle of sheets on the bed. The stench of cheap perfume hung thick on the air.

Wayland drew a breath and bellowed. "Everyone in the front room now!"

The two girls came alert, their eyes wide with fright. They were both young, their lurid makeup smeared, their hair tousled. They sat upright in the bed, clutching the sheets to their naked bodies. They saw Travis Wayland's thunderous expression and squealed.

"Get up, you bastards!" Wayland snarled at the soldiers on the floor. One of the men lay on his back snoring loudly, his face covered by a pair of red satin panties. Wayland snatched up the undergarments and kicked him hard in the shins. He came awake in a fit of phlegmy coughing.

"Get up, you bastards! Now!"

The farmhouse filled with groans and exclamations of chaotic confusion. Wayland heard the thunder of heavy boots descending stairs. He went back out into the front room and saw three men coming down from the upper story, each of them fumbling to button clothing and rouse themselves into wakefulness.

"Who the fuck…?"

"I'm Lieutenant Travis Wayland. Who the fuck are you?" his voice cracked like a whip.

The men snapped to attention at the foot of the stairs. Wayland eyed them with malevolent menace.

"Sergeant Nossiter, sir," the closest man answered, his eyes straight ahead, staring in wide-eyed shock at the window

Wayland had thrown a chair through. He was a short, nuggety man with oily black hair and dark eyes.

"Sergeant Rye, sir," the next said. He had a crop of short wiry red hair and a hooked nose. His nervous eyes darted to Wayland's face, and he smiled weakly.

"And you?" Wayland demanded of the man at the end of the line.

"Sergeant First Class McGrath," the soldier replied. After a moment of deliberate impudence, he added, "sir." He looked like a hard man. He had a square jaw, broad shoulders and a powerful physique that strained the seams of his uniform.

Wayland ignored the first two men and stood toe-to-toe with McGrath.

"Did you know about this?" he flung his arm in a violent gesture that encompassed the entire room and all its bedlam.

"Yes, sir."

"And you allowed it?" Wayland was furious.

"The men were given a twenty-four hour furlough, Lieutenant."

"To get themselves blind drunk in the middle of a war?"

"None of the men are drunk, Lieutenant," the Sergeant didn't give a damn about trying to impress his new officer. He stood unflinching and his eyes remained level. "They're exhausted. They only shared a few beers and a couple of bottles."

"Then how do you explain this?" Wayland held up the pair of red lace panties.

There was a heartbeat of stony silence. Sergeant McGrath looked closely at the frilly undergarments. He shook his head and said straight-faced, "They're not mine, sir."

Wayland blinked. For a moment the room seemed stunned by the Platoon Sergeant's delicate insolence. Then someone began to laugh. Wayland wheeled on the man, his eyes blazing but the offending tanker disguised the sound into a hacking cough.

"There are two naked women in a bedroom down the hall, Sergeant!"

For a moment McGrath appeared mystified, then his face lit up into an expression of sweet angelic innocence. "Those two young ladies are from the local convent, sir. They arrived here late last night in the pouring rain. It seems their little donkey broke its leg and couldn't pull their cart filled with donations for the children's orphanage back to church. We offered the nuns a place to spend the night where they would be safe, and where they could dry their clothes."

"You're lying."

"That might be so, sir, but I'm prepared to swear it's the truth."

The Sergeant's flinty unflinching stare spoke the real truth. The behavior and the performance of the platoon were his responsibility and it was none of Wayland's damned business. He, McGrath, would make sure the crews went into battle ready and willing to fight. Wayland had to concede grudging respect for the man. McGrath was exactly the kind of Platoon Sergeant he himself had been until just a couple of weeks ago.

Some of the tension went from the room. "What's the status of the tanks?"

"The men worked on them throughout last night, sir, overhauling equipment and triple-checking every system. They're dirty, ugly and unsightly… but every one of those vehicles is ready to fight a war."

Wayland grunted. He gave the men assembled around the edge of the room a final, withering glare.

"Very good, Sergeant. I want everyone assembled out front for a full inspection in ten minutes," he flicked McGrath a wintry glare. "And I want those two naked nuns sent back to the convent immediately."

*

The men formed a ragged line in front of the barn. They were unkempt and bleary-eyed. The wind came buffeting from the east, flattening the grass on the hill and thrashing the branches above their heads. Dark clouds seemed to scrape against the skyline.

And then the storm broke. Thunder rolled across the heavens and a fork of lightning lit the gloom. Wayland felt the first raindrops splash against his shoulders. Suddenly the air filled with a pearly misted downpour.

The men in the ranks grumbled. Sergeant Nossiter muttered a growl of complaint out the side of his mouth. "Christ!" he moaned. "We'll fucking freeze to death. How are we expected to fight the Russians if this bastard gives us pneumonia?"

Sergeant McGrath was smiling. Just smiling.

Wayland paced down the line, stopping to speak to several men. Most of them were uncomfortable and wary, guarding their apprehension behind 'yes, sir, no, sir,' answers. None of them had seen combat before. The faces that stared back at him seemed very, very young – and with that realization came the crushing weight of responsibility that had been hoisted onto Wayland's shoulders. He had never sought promotion, and his battlefield commission had brought no elation. Now the full burden of what that promotion entailed struck him. He wanted to be a good officer, but he knew the dangers of trying to be liked by the men he commanded. These were young soldiers he would have to lead into battle, and a firefight was not the place for a friendly, approachable commander. First they would have to hate him, because loyalty and obedience only ever came from respect.

He reached the end of the line and stepped back. "My name is Wayland," he told the platoon, "Lieutenant Travis Wayland, and I've been a soldier since I was eighteen years old," he paused for a moment. The faces staring back at him remained blank. "I fought at the Battle of the 73rd Easting and I fought across the Middle East – and I've fought against the Russians; the same enemy you are preparing to fight against right now at the Battle of Jekabpils just two weeks ago.

"And until that battle I was a Platoon Sergeant, like Sergeant McGrath." He saw the sudden surprise on several faces; a moment of wide-eyed disbelief. A ripple of muttered noise ran down the line. "So I know what it's like to stand where you are standing. I know what it's like to be face-down in the mud when bullets are flying around your head – and I know what it's like to be in a tank when enemy armor is trying to kill you." He paused for a moment and let his words resonate. The rain eased abruptly, but the wind across the slope cut like a knife through their sodden clothing.

He pointed away to the east. The artillery barrage had stopped and the light from their gunfire no longer flickered on the skyline, but the smoke scar across the horizon remained, mingling into the brooding cloud-filled sky. "The same Russian soldiers I fought in Lithuania two weeks ago are now driving towards Warsaw. They're less than a hundred miles in that direction. That's a three hour drive. They're that close. And they're fighting hard." Some of the men turned their heads and stared as though they expected to see a column of T-90s suddenly burst across the farm fields. "They're good. They're tough. They are well lead – and they think they're unbeatable. Our job is to prove that we're better. It's up to us to defend this place and smash the enemy to pieces."

He had their attention. They might not like the message, but they understood the simple brutal truth of the situation. "Your best chance of surviving this war is to do your job well and trust the men around you."

The wind died down, then came back with a vengeance. A bolt of lightning split the gloom and thunder rumbled.

"When we get into battle, we target the enemy's command vehicles first. You all know this from your training. But I'm telling you that in the real world, when you're in the midst of a firefight, it really does matter. It's not just some military academy's theory. Target the enemy's command vehicles and you sever the head from the snake. The Russian tankers aren't trained as well as you are, and they're not trained to think for themselves. They're closely controlled, their tactics rely on structure and overwhelming numbers. The Russian equipment might have changed over the years, but their fighting mentality has not. Their doctrine is the same as it was in the Second World War. So when a command vehicle crosses your sights, you kill the bastards. It's the quickest way to win. With one kill you can render an entire tank platoon or company temporarily ineffective."

A couple of men shuffled their feet and looked anxious. The wind caught an open door inside the farmhouse and slammed it shut suddenly with a loud 'crack!' like a gunshot.

"I know you've been well trained and that you're good soldiers," Wayland went on. "There's nothing I can teach you. But I can show you how to be killers; how to win. Because if you don't win, you'll die. It's as simple as that," he explained harshly. "You may never like me – I couldn't care less. But you better listen to me. Because any day now we're going to be in a fight for our lives, and I'm your best chance of surviving. Any questions?"

Silence.

"Sergeant McGrath?"

"Sir?"

"Make sure every bustle rack is packed properly and that every tank is carrying a full load of fuel and ammunition."

"Sir."

Dismissed, the men made a dash for the shelter of the porch. The sudden far-away sound of a revving engine made Wayland turn. A Humvee was bouncing along the mud trail, coming closer.

Chapter 2:

"Are you Wayland?" Captain Ewart Kohn swung the passenger door of the Humvee wide and jumped down into the mud before the vehicle had come to a complete halt.

"Yes, sir," Wayland saluted.

Captain Kohn returned the salute absently and stared up into the sky. "Christ! This is the last damned thing we need." He shook himself like a spaniel and swept his eyes around the farmhouse. Some of the tankers were drifting inside the building. Others, under Sergeant McGrath's instruction, were carrying haversacks and boxes of MREs.

The Captain saw the barn and motioned Wayland towards it, then had to double back to the Humvee to retrieve a sheaf of pages. He was in an ebullient, energized mood, his voice loud with enthusiasm.

"We've got a mission!" he smiled and waved the papers in his hand to reveal a wad of notes, satellite photos and maps. "We're going head on against the Russians."

"We are, sir?" Wayland winced. "When?"

"Today!" He strode to a bale of hay and laid out the satellite images. He was a man in his late thirties with a halo of wispy blonde hair atop a face of unremarkable features. "We're advancing to a village called Stare Lubiejewo," he unfolded a map of northern Poland. "It's about eighty clicks northeast. The nearest town is called Ostrow Mazowiecka," he mangled the pronunciation.

"And the Russians, sir?" Wayland leaned close and peered at the map.

"They're here," Kohn described a vague circle around Lomza. "The Russians overwhelmed the town's defenses a couple of days ago. Now they're driving southwest towards us. Stare Lubiejewo straddles one of the roads they need to take to advance on Warsaw. We're going to get to the village first and defend it for as long as possible."

"That's a lot to ask of a Company of Abrams tanks, sir," Wayland sounded doubtful. It sounded like a suicide mission.

"We'll be reinforced," Captain Kohn said airily.

"We will, sir?"

"Of course."

"By who?"

Irritated by the question and galled by his new Lieutenant's apparent lack of enthusiasm for fighting, Kohn's voice became snappy. "By those forces deemed necessary by command sufficient to the task of fortifying our position, Lieutenant."

"Yes, sir."

His enthusiastic mood dampened, the Captain's voice turned churlish. "Your Platoon will move out immediately and make for the village. Command rushed a company of British infantry into the settlement last night – Number Two Company, 1st Battalion of the Irish Guards. They're light infantry but their anti-tank platoon is equipped with Javelins," he rummaged through his notes until he found the paperwork. "They're commanded by a Major Bernard Browne. When you reach the village, you are to liaise with the Irish to co-ordinate a defensive perimeter. All this information will be uploaded digitally for you to study on your tank's CID, including waypoints and the latest intel on Russian positions. I'll also do a sand-table with your platoon before you set out."

A 'sand-table' briefing was a visual mock up map of the mission area modelled onto the ground using dirt, sand, rocks and even twigs and lengths of twine to represent terrain features. The briefing gave everyone from the lowest ranking privates to the officers involved a visual walk-through of the mission, the objectives and the terrain's unique tactical features. Some of the sand-tables Wayland had seen during his Army career had been little more than crudely drawn lines gouged from the sunbaked earth, while others he remembered had been miniature sand-sculpted works of art.

"And the rest of the company, sir? When can we expect support?"

"We will be following, Lieutenant. I expect we will reach your position by mid-afternoon. Your task is to hold Stare Lubiejewo with the Irish until we arrive."

"Should that prove difficult, sir?"

"That depends on the Russians, Lieutenant," Kohn said acidly. "The latest satellite and HUMINT reports suggest Russian motorized infantry are racing ahead of the main spearhead, probably trying to seize the village before we can fortify it."

Wayland nodded his head. It was a suicide mission.

Captain Kohn seemed to sense Wayland's reticence and regarded him with a challenging tilt of his head. "Are you frightened, Lieutenant? I was told you had a reputation for bold action and daring."

"No man in their right mind looks forward to a battle, Captain."

"I am. I can't wait to fight the Russians… but I doubt you have any reason for serious concern. I don't think the enemy will reach the village before nightfall."

"That suits me fine, sir." Wayland said.

The Captain turned and paced the straw-covered ground. The roof leaked in a dozen places, dripping water in puddles. He stopped and sketched a couple of lines in the dirt with the toe of his boot, frowning. Suddenly he wheeled round.

"I've been waiting my whole career for this moment," he said vehemently. "I just hope the Russians don't reach the town before I get there for the fight."

Wayland felt a ripple of unease but suppressed the reaction. "Maybe the Russians will wait until you get into position before they launch their assault, sir," he said laconically.

The Captain, evidently not detecting the irony in Wayland's voice looked up. "God, I hope so," he said with fervor.

*

Ten miles northeast of Warsaw, the column of four Abrams tanks struck a straggling mass of refugees fleeing the battlefront. Military Police were in the midst of the fray, their Humvees parked by a stand of trees. They were trying to herd the civilians onto one side of the road to keep a lane open for military vehicles.

Wayland, viewing the scene from the commander's hatch in the turret of the tank, stared with astonishment. The road north was choked with an eclectic collection of slow-moving passenger vehicles, small trucks, people on bicycles and those forced to walk. Women and children trudged along the muddy blacktop, worn down under the weight of their burdens. Those too sick or weak to walk were being pushed in two-wheeled handcarts, or carried on litters. Children cried. They were drab, downcast figures, many carrying their belongings on their backs. The cars were loaded down with pieces of furniture and bags of clothing, the entire length of the column plodding through a grey haze of exhaust fumes and light rain showers. Farm lorries carried people packed together like cattle in an abattoir truck, their eyes blank and haunted.

The MPs were overwhelmed. They had erected barricades to herd the column into one lane, but the diversion had simply been ignored. Now the soldiers were standing with weapons drawn, their faces tight with tension, barking instructions at the refugees who shuffled aside with bovine lethargy for a few paces only to swell back across the full width of the road once they were past the checkpoint.

Wayland slowed his Abrams to a halt and the masses washed around the tank. A harassed MP Sergeant came wading through the wall of human misery and clambered onto the Abram's hull. His face was pale and sweating. "Where are you headed?"

"Stare Lubiejewo," Wayland said.

"Christ! The entire fucking Russian Army is heading that way."

"Yeah, I know."

"Where's the rest of your Battalion?"

"It's just us."

The MP blinked in horror and his expression became one reserved for the condemned man on his way to the gallows.

"Your only chance to reach Stare Lubiejewo before nightfall is to get off the road. This column of refugees stretches all the way to Wyszkow." He drew a map with his fingertip in the dusty steel of the tank's turret. "The bridge over the Bug River is clear – we just got word from another checkpoint at a little place called Tumanek. But until you reach that bridge you're in for long delays unless you go cross-country."

Wayland spoke across the Platoon net and the tanks conducted a 'Short Halt' to clear the road, ploughing into soft rain-soaked fields. They pushed on, their speed slowed, their passage marked by a hail of spattered mud thrown high into the air by the churning tracks.

They skirted the fringes of Wyszkow and bumped back onto the blacktop, the vehicles painted thick with mud and dirt.

Wayland glanced at his watch and cursed. The sky overhead began clearing, the heavy rainclouds moving west, pushed by a stiffening breeze. Patches of blue sky showed through the wind-shredded cloud front – but in their place grew a darkening stain of smoke, drawn like a black ugly smear across the northern horizon.

The tanks were travelling in a column with Rye's Abrams leading followed by Wayland, McGrath and Nossiter. Wayland called Rye on the radio.

"Red Two, this is One. Kick it in the ass, we don't have all day."

The column of Abrams raced ahead. The road reached a crest and beyond the rise revealed a bridge over a winding river. Parked across the approach to the bridge were three US Cavalry Strykers.

Wayland halted the Abrams column under the curious gaze of the Cavalrymen. One of the men, an officer, strode towards the tanks with a bemused expression on his face. "I sure hope you boys are lost and just looking for directions."

"Afraid not," Wayland leaned down from the turret hatch.

The cavalry officer's eyebrows lifted, his face became a frown. "You're here on purpose?"

"Gotta be somewhere," Wayland said.

"Yeah, well that 'somewhere' should be anywhere but here, bud. The entire fuckin' Russian Army is at the end of this road."

"I know," Wayland said. "That's where we are heading, and we're in a hurry."

The cavalry officer had a Texan drawl and a suntanned face. He narrowed his eyes and regarded Wayland shrewdly. "Well you're going to have to hurry up and wait for about ten minutes," he jerked his thumb back over his shoulder. "I've got a mechanical issue. Shouldn't take much longer."

Wayland spoke across the platoon net and the tanks pulled to the shoulder of the road. He climbed down from his vehicle and introduced himself to the cavalry officer. The two men shook hands.

"Have you had contact with the enemy?"

"We've been scouting forward for the last two days. The Russians are still concentrated around Lomza, but there's a couple of motorized infantry companies and maybe a company of T-90s pushing forward. We broke off contact this morning."

Wayland frowned. "Any idea where they were heading?"

"This way," the cavalry officer said ominously.

Wayland let the tank crews wander into the fields to relieve themselves and stretch their legs. He dropped down in the grass with his back against a tree and thought about the task they had been ordered to undertake. He wondered about the quality of his men, and how they would respond to the brutal shock of a firefight. Sergeant McGrath squatted down on his haunches and plucked at a long stem of weeds.

"I heard about you in Afghanistan," he said casually.

"Oh?"

"Yeah. I heard a story. Wasn't sure if it was true or not."

"Ask me. I'll tell you."

"It was about some kids…"

Wayland nodded his head and a shadow seemed to pass across his eyes. "Yeah. It happened," he said. His expression became distant. Then the words came, faltering at first, like a nightmare being relived. "My platoon of Abrams were on the outskirts of Asadabad in the Ghaziabad District of Kunar province. We were on patrol supporting Afghan security forces. The day before Taliban insurgents had attacked an ANA checkpoint.

"We were patrolling a warren of narrow laneways with the tanks providing overwatch when a handful of local kids came running out onto the road directly ahead of my tank. Every one of them was armed with an AK-47. My gunner asked me if he should fire. The kids were aiming their weapons at us.

"I hesitated. Then the gunner cried out, 'RPG! RPG! Eight o'clock!'

"I spun around in the turret and saw a kid against a wall with a weapon aimed at us. He was about fifty yards away. Instinct said to give the order to shoot but intuition told me something wasn't right. I told my gunner to hold his fire and held my breath. Ten seconds later the Afghani security forces cornered eight kids in a nearby alleyway. The 'weapons' were all plastic toys. The Taliban had given the replicas to the children to play with in the hope they would be gunned down by American troops, causing a major scandal in the media…"

"Yeah," McGrath nodded. "That's how I heard it." The moment seemed like a weighing and measurement of character. Sergeant McGrath looked out across the field.

"They'll do alright," he said, changing the subject. He nodded at the tankers. "They're good. Lieutenant Smith trained them right, you'll see."

Wayland grunted.

"Some of them are just kids," he smiled with a kind of fond pride. "But every one of them knows their job. What they don't know about… sir…. is you."

"Meaning?"

"They don't know what kind of leader you are. This company has already got enough gung-ho cowboy officers, eager to make a name for themselves. They're impulsive – reckless. They're dangerous."

"Kohn?"

"The Captain's out to prove himself," McGrath warned. "He comes from a military family. His old man commanded an infantry company in the 101st Airborne during the Vietnam War and earned a Silver Star at the Battle of Hamburger Hill. And he's got a couple of step-brothers. One was a scout during Desert Storm. The other was a Marine Sergeant who fought in Iraq during the second Battle of Fallujah. Both of 'em earned Bronze Stars. That's a hell of a long shadow to live in, y'know?"

"That explains why he's so eager for action."

"The men are wondering if you're another cowboy. They know you've got combat experience, but some men are forced to fight, and others go looking for a fight, you know what I mean? The men want to know what kind of combat veteran you are, and how many other soldiers you got killed while you were earning your reputation."

Wayland could have taken the veiled accusation as an insult. But he sensed the Sergeant's comments were born out of simple, absolute sincerity.

"You can let the men know," he said reasonably, "that I'm not here for glory, and I never take chances unless the odds are in my favor. I fight because I have to – but when I fight, I expect to win."

*

They reached the outskirts of Stare Lubiejewo just after noon. Wayland had the ominous sense that he was driving towards a storm. The skyline ahead of the racing tanks grew portentously darker as thick roiling clouds of smoke filled the far horizon.

The approach to the village was along a dual-carriageway road, lined by a wall of trees that offered only fleeting views of the land to either side. What little Wayland saw was rich farmland with rows of newly-planted crops that seemed to stretch for miles across flat featureless terrain.

The road was deserted. They drove past a hotel set back from the main thoroughfare at the end of a wide parking lot and Wayland was surprised to see several parked cars near the driveway. A few hundred yards further on they reached an intersection. Wayland braked to a stop. The road north continued to Lomza and the Russian Army. The intersecting east-west road led to a nest of tree-studded local streets lined with homes, shops and schools.

Wayland flung up his binoculars and studied the road north. It was low country, edged on the horizon by a line of gentle hills on which were dotted clumps of green trees. The fields in the foreground were fringed with low hedgerows. Some of the land was under the plough. Other patches in the quilt of colors were fields of long dry grass. He could see no sign of approaching Russians; no movement on the road at all. He ordered Sergeant Nossiter's tank west along the suburban side-street. "Keep your eyes on the northern skyline," he ordered over the platoon net. Then he sent Sergeant Rye's Abrams east into the narrow village laneways with the same instructions.

He climbed down from his tank and beckoned Sergeant McGrath from his Abrams with a wave of his arm. "There's supposed to be a company of Irish Infantry somewhere around here. You can help me find them."

Chapter 3:

The village was sprinkled with an assortment of quaint, simple houses on either side of tree-studded lanes. Many of the homes stood on wide fenced plots of ground given over to gardens or small crops. Wayland walked past some kind of agricultural trade school that looked like a set of bleak multi-story apartment blocks.

Two men appeared from inside a ground-floor doorway and came striding towards Wayland and McGrath purposefully.

"Lieutenant Wayland?" the voice was soft, the accent unmistakably Irish behind an engaging easy manner.

"Major Browne?"

The Irish officer had a thin handsome face; his features chiseled with deep cut lines on either side of his mouth and across his brow. His eyes were shrewd and intelligent, his short sandy hair meticulously trimmed and combed. He was immaculately dressed, and around his neck he wore the elegant eccentric affectation of a green cravat. He looked at Wayland with a friendly smile. The man following was tall and slim, his face somehow ageless. He had dark hair and bruises of sleep-deprived fatigue beneath his eyes.

Wayland and the Major shook hands briefly.

"Well, it's a bloody shambles, Wayland. An utter bloody shambles," Major Browne sighed bitterly. "I'm contacting my Battalion HQ and withdrawing my men. This little bloody village isn't worth fighting for."

"Major?"

"Not a damned pub anywhere!" the Major voiced his pantomimed outrage. "Not a one. Can you believe it? Only the bloody Polish would build an entire village and forget to make space for a pub. Christ on his cross! The best they can muster is a bloody wine bar in the local hotel. A few bottles of port and a Riesling that's barely good enough to degrease an engine block with. How in the hell are brave fighting men expected to leaven war's rigors without a pint of Gat?"

Wayland smiled. He took an instant liking to the Irishman, though he found the rapid speech and the lilting cadence a challenge to follow. He felt himself leaning closer, trying to catch every word.

"It sounds like your men have endured dreadful hardship, Major."

"Your compassion for our plight is noted, Lieutenant," Major Browne said with melodramatic gravity. "Coming from anyone other than a great combat hero such as yourself, I would have taken your words as cynicism. However far be it from me to doubt the honor of a man recently commissioned on the battlefield. We heard about your exploits. Congratulations on your promotion. Meritorious, almost suicidal bravery, eh? You must be part Irish."

"Maybe, sir," Wayland grinned.

The Major nodded acknowledgement to Sergeant McGrath and turned to introduce the man behind him.

"This is Captain O'Malley. He's an absolute scoundrel and not to be trusted with money or women. But he's grand with a gun, so he is."

The Irish Captain inclined his head and smiled with good-humored indulgence.

Wayland gestured. "And this is Sergeant First Class McGrath, the Platoon Sergeant." More smiles, more nodded greetings. The introductions completed the four men settled down to the business of war.

Major Browne took Wayland and McGrath on a tour of the settlement, pointing out the tactical weak points and the disposition of his men. "I must say, we're bloody glad to have you here, so we are," the Major spoke as he walked. "The rest of your company will be along shortly?"

"Sometime during the afternoon," Wayland said.

Browne winced. "Well let's hope nothing delays them," Browne said.

"Do you know something I don't, Major?"

Browne stopped and tapped the side of his nose. "My da was born with the second sight, Lieutenant. He could see the future. And I think I've inherited his gift. Naturally, God speaks directly to all Irishmen because we're his chosen people – and he's been talking to me all morning," the Major went on. "Bernard, he says. Bernard, lad. Are you daft? Get your men back to Warsaw. The Russians are coming."

Wayland arched his eyebrows. "And did God happen to mention an estimated time of arrival?"

The Irish Major shook his head. "No. But I can smell 'em, Lieutenant. They're closer than we'd like them to be, and they'll be here sooner than we want."

Most of the Irish Guards company were positioned in buildings along the western flank of the village with the anti-tank platoon dug in close to the intersection. The eastern end of the village faced onto a vast, dense forest; Browne had left that flank only lightly defended. "The Ruskies aren't going to come at us in single file through the forest," the Major justified his decision. "They'll want to overwhelm us quickly so they'll need room to maneuver. My guess is they'll attack to the west where the ground is open, and they can come at us in force."

Wayland nodded. "What about the local population?"

"They're mad as bloody hatters," the Major answered. "Stubborn as mules."

"You've had trouble evacuating them?"

"Aye. Some have fled to Warsaw, but the rest of them want to stay and fight. They've barricaded themselves in their homes and they won't feckin leave! There's an old codger down that street," he pointed, "armed with a pitchfork and a shotgun. Says he was born in the village and he'll die here. And there are at least a dozen more like him. Others are incapable of evacuating because they're completely bollocksed."

"Bollocksed?"

"Off their tits, Lieutenant. Stocious. Pissed off their faces."

"What about women and children?"

"Aye, most have taken their wee ones back to Warsaw, but there's nothing I can do about the ones who refused to evacuate. I don't have the men or time to spare."

They reached the intersection where Wayland and McGrath's tanks were parked and turned to stare along the route north from where the Russians were expected. The road was deserted.

"Where do you want us?" Wayland asked.

Major Browne pointed. "There's good cover behind that house. From there you'll have a view away to the west, across the farm fields. And there's a hull down position behind that brick wall that will defend the road…"

Wayland nodded. They walked to inspect the firing positions and passed a narrow alley. There were half-a-dozen bodies slumped in the gutter. They lay in the litter and filth, insensible. They had drunk themselves into a stupor instead of joining the stream of refugees fleeing from the fighting. Now there was nothing that could be done for them.

Standing at the entrance to the alley, Major Browne shrugged. "I told you. It's bloody hopeless."

The four men walked back to where the tanks were parked. Captain O'Malley and Wayland exchanged radio frequencies, so the tanks and infantry could log into the new SDR (Software Defined Radio) system still being introduced to NATO troops. The software would allow Wayland's tank to monitor the Irish infantry company's radio frequency and 1st Platoon's internal frequency, while the rest of the Abrams' in the Platoon monitored their own company's frequency and the 1st Platoon's internal frequency.

Wayland and the Major left the others at the intersection and went forward alone, wandering down the center of the road, the closest men to the approaching danger. When they were out of earshot from the others, they stopped and stared into the distance.

"When the Russians come down this road, all hell is going to break loose," Wayland said quietly.

"Aye," Major Browne agreed. "We're not going to be able to hold them for long – not if they come at us in force."

"Do you have a fallback position?"

"No. My orders are to hold the village."

Wayland grunted. "Mine too. But if they come at us with armor and APCs at the same time..?"

Major Browne gave a fatalistic smile. "Well, God's an Irishman, so I know my men and I will prevail. But I'm afraid you're fucked!"

It was a last moment of levity in what threatened to be an afternoon of horror and killing. They were about to wander back to the intersection when Wayland detected a fresh smudge of smoke beyond a low rise of hills. He peered into the distance, his eyes squinted, and as he did the smoke seemed to thicken.

The radio on the Major's hip squawked and a voice through the static said urgently, "Sandman Six, Dublin Three on the school rooftop. Enemy in sight!"

"Christ!" Major Browne cursed. "We've run out of time."

The Russians had come to Stare Lubiejewo, and now the killing would begin.

*

Major Browne ran for the ground-floor doors of the technical school, past his British Army command Landrover in the carpark. Wayland was right on his heels. They stormed the building's internal stairwell, pounding the steps two at a time. They burst out onto the rooftop breathing hard.

There were four British infantrymen on the roof. Two snipers were posted at the corners of the building facing to the north, and two more men were set back from the roofline. Browne dashed to the two men hunched over a small control panel.

"What have you got?"

The Corporal holding the monitor screen offered it to the Major. "A dozen or more Russian troop carriers, sir," the young soldier said. "They look like BMP-3s."

Browne studied the image carefully. The picture was being sent back to the rooftop by a palm-sized surveillance drone called a Black Hornet. The UAV weighted just a few ounces and was standard issue to British units. With a range of around two kilometers and a flying time of almost thirty minutes, the pocket-sized drone was one of the smallest operating systems in the world.

Browne stared down into the monitor. The seven-inch LCD screen showed a wide stretch of farm fields. Around the edges of the screen were data readouts, showing the drone's direction, altitude and flying time.

"We're at the limit of our range, sir, about two k's north of our position," the young Corporal explained. He was operating the drone with a handheld controller that looked like a TV remote control.

From the UAV's position and height, Browne could see far to the north and northwest. At the limit of the camera's range a trail of dust seemed to be moving steadily closer.

"Zoom in."

The image tightened onto three vehicles, made grainy by distance, moving along the ridge of a low crest. The APCs were flinging up mud and water from the rain-soaked ground. The lead vehicle jounced over a patch of broken ground and disappeared behind a billow of dust and dirt.

"Pan left and zoom out," the Major ordered.

The image changed. More low-profiled BMP-3s filled the screen, and near a patch of dense woods, Browne thought he could detect the silhouette of a tank, though it was impossible from the small image to determine its type. He handed the monitor back to the Corporal and caught Wayland's eye.

"Fifteen, maybe twenty Russian APCs approaching from the northwest," he said. "They're not using the road – they're coming at us across country. And there might be armor supporting them from elevated ground about three kilometers away," he frowned.

"Christ," Wayland breathed.

"Yes, quite," Major Browne understated the looming threat. "I think we're in for a fight, Lieutenant. This might be a good time to return to your Abrams. Life is about to get bloody dangerous."

*

Lieutenant Colonel Pugacheva, hero of the wars in Georgia and Afghanistan, Order of Saint George 4th class medal recipient, and lion of Chechnya and the Caucasus campaigns, stood beside his command vehicle on a low wooded rise north of Stare Lubiejewo, and belched loudly. He moved his tongue around his mouth getting the taste of it before he spoke.

"There is a Platoon of American Abrams tanks in the village," he lowered his binoculars.

"Four tanks will not slow our progress, Colonel," Alferov, the Russian Battalion's zampolit said scornfully.

"Four American tanks," Pugacheva said, "are enough to tear an ill-considered operation to pieces, Alferov. I've seen it happen."

The Colonel had a flat, scarred face, his features fleshy, his eyebrows wild and wiry beneath a shock of grey hair. He turned to the Political Officer accusingly. "You told me the village would be defended by only a handful of infantry."

Alferov shrugged his shoulders. The Battalion's zampolit was a cunning, clever man with sinister connections to Moscow.

He had travelled forward with the Battalion Tactical Group to oversee the attack on the village. In Soviet times, every unit commander had a zampolit deputy who represented the Communist Party and could veto any of the commander's decisions. In 2018 the position had been reintroduced to the Russian military apparatus. Technically, the zampolit was responsible for the patriotic spirit and moral of the soldiers. In reality, their influence was so pervasive and insidious, that even grizzled Lieutenant Colonels like Pugacheva were wary of the malevolent influence they wielded.

The Colonel despised the zampolit, and despised, too, the need to co-opt battlefield command decisions to a Political Officer – a man with no combat experience and no military training. "You told me it was a handful of infantry. You made no mention of tanks," the Colonel repeated the accusation.

"A platoon of Abrams?" Alferov sounded dismissive. "Our attack will roll right over them."

"Attack?" Pugacheva barked. "Half my force is still stranded on the roads south from Lomza."

His force comprised a motorized rifle battalion in BMP-3 troop carriers with two companies of T-90 tanks in support. So far only two companies of motorized infantry and a single company of tanks had reached the staging point for the assault.

"You're suggesting caution? A delay?" the Political Officer dangled the words like a dangerous dare. Pugacheva heard the menace in the zampolit's voice and deigned to explain himself.

"I have already fought in this war," the Colonel reminded Alferov acidly. "I know what the NATO troops are capable of. They're tough bastards when they're defending built-up positions. If we charge at them half-cocked, they'll give us a bloody nose."

"They have four tanks and a handful of men, Colonel," Alferov's voice was pitiless. "You have over twenty BMPs, several hundred elite Russian troops, and over a dozen tanks. And might I remind you, Colonel, that you are the pointed tip of Russia's spearhead into Poland. You are the forward-most commander. Our people look to you in this moment to display the traits of a Russian warrior, not behave like some callow boy afraid of the enemy," his tone dripped with contempt. "Or would you wait until the rest of the Tactical Group arrives? Do you need more men, even more armor? Will you feel safe attacking the little village with another dozen BMPs and another dozen tanks?" he mocked.

"They have the advantage of being behind prepared defenses…"

"They're not!" the zampolit put steel into his voice. "The tanks were not there when our scouts reported back at dawn. They are newly arrived."

"Perhaps we should reconnoiter the village more carefully. It is dangerous to advance without the support of artillery."

"Perhaps I should place a call to Army Command and report your timidity to the President's office," Alferov poured scorn on the Colonel and smiled a secret, dangerous smile. "Other such hesitant commanders have been shot for cowardice during this campaign already. Would you prefer to spend your last moments staring down a firing squad rather than fighting the enemy?" he let the thinly veiled threat hang in the air.

Lieutenant Colonel Pugacheva was a grizzled veteran, but somewhere along the line, Alferov decided, the man had lost his appetite for war; lost the savage instinct of the warrior. It would be better to contact Moscow and have him replaced, but time prohibited such a move. It was critical the village be secured quickly so the main column's advance on Warsaw continued uninhibited. So instead the old Colonel must be taunted into action.

"Every moment you delay the attack brings shame upon your family and your reputation," the Political Officer goaded the Colonel with impunity. Already, the dispatch he would write to Moscow was taking shape in his head, a dispatch that would end Pugacheva's military career. And if, for some reason, the attack on the village failed, the report would become an unofficial death warrant.

The Colonel realized he was backed into a corner by the insidious power this evil little man possessed to destroy, on a whim, a thirty year career of dedicated service. He sighed heavily.

"Very well," he tried to put purpose into his voice. "We'll attack immediately. The motorized infantry will drive for the western edge of the settlement with the tank company held back to cover their advance. Once the infantry has a foothold on the village outskirts, we'll send the T-90s forward to finish the job."

*

"All Red elements, this is Red One. Battle carry HEAT and report REDCON status!" Wayland barked across the Platoon net, demanding a readiness report from every vehicle.

As the REDCON status replies came in, he ordered his driver forward until the vehicle was partially concealed behind the side-wall of an abandoned house, then watched Sergeant McGrath's Abrams made a three-point turn until it was hull-down behind a brick wall, covering the main road.

From his position, Wayland could see Red Three at the end of the western edge of the village. Sergeant Nossiter had reversed the Abrams in between two houses. He could also see across the open fields, all the way to the tree-lined ridge in the distance. He watched anxiously. Behind the rise of ground a cloud of dust was boiling like the smoke of a forest fire. The Russians were behind that ridge, forming up and preparing to attack.

The seconds ticked by. Wayland checked the tank's BMS. The Battlefield Management System was the US Army's FBCB2, designed to reduce the fog of war by giving fighting units a digital display of all friendly forces. It also plotted the position of enemy units as they appeared. The image was superimposed above a map of the local terrain, displaying a two-mile square of ground with the Platoon's four tanks in the middle.

Wayland drew a deep breath. He cast his eyes around the interior. His crew were at their stations, poised like sprinters at the starter's gun.

On the edge of the BMS a red icon appeared to the northwest of their position, then another and another. Wayland peered through the view ports built into his commander's cupola and saw the horizon fill with a swarm of Russian armored personnel carriers.

"Red, Red One. Engage at will!"

One minute the crest of the far ridge was littered with Russian BMP-3s and the next they were concealed behind swirling grey-white smoke that enveloped the fields in a blanket of haze.

"HEAT up!" The tank's loader, Specialist Wayne Swan yelled to alert the gunner there was already a HEAT round loaded into the breach.

Wayland saw a BMP-3 emerge from a haze of smoke through his CITV and snapped the order. "Designate PC!" He thumbed a button on his commander's override handle causing the tank's turret to automatically slew directly onto the target.

"Identified!" Gunner J.J. Brown engaged the target and centered the sight reticle. He stabbed the laser button with his thumb and a thin beam of light reached out for the target. Instantly the range display flashed up on his sight. The Abrams sophisticated fire control took over, plotting target distance and elevating the barrel. It took the computer another split-second to calculate air density and humidity, and to measure the wind's speed and its direction.

"Fire and adjust!" Wayland gave the command.

J.J. crushed the trigger. "On the way!"

The Abrams rocked on its suspension as the first shell left the barrel at the end of a thirty-foot muzzle blast.

The projectile struck the BMP-3 front on. Inside the Russian APC, the driver was just in the process of crashing through a hedgerow. The impact of the round blew the vehicle to pieces in a fireball of flames and boiling black smoke, killing the crew and the infantry inside in an instant. The sound of the explosion rumbled across the sky.

"Target!" J.J declared.

But there were over a dozen more BMP-3s advancing, racing at high speed towards the village. Wayland heard the loud 'crack!' of Nossiter's tank firing and saw the flaming tongue of the muzzle-blast from the corner of his eye. A second later a fireball flared through the distant smoke away to the west of his position.

The BMP-3 was the mainstay of the Russian motorized infantry force; a wedge-fronted steel box on tracks. With a crew of three and the capacity to carry up to nine infantry inside its hull, the BMP-3 was one of the most heavily armed infantry combat vehicles in service. But its protective armor was no match for the powerful punch of an Abrams tank. In quick succession two more of the Russian APCs were blown apart, reduced to shrapnel and a towering billow of black oily smoke. The long grass in the farm fields caught fire, adding to the smoke and confusion.

"HEAT, Swanny!"

"Up!"

"Identified PC!" JJ's voice sounded unnaturally calm in Wayland's CVC. The gunner thumbed the weapon's distance lasers.

The Abrams turret turned and the barrel lowered an inch.

"Fire!"

"On the way!"

The sound of the shot going downrange drowned out the clamor of the battle. The target vehicle blew open and the tremor of its violent explosion seemed to shake the air. Shrapnel was flung a hundred feet into the air, the crew and the infantry inside immolated.

Wayland set his sights on a BMP bulldozing its way through a field of tall dry grass and called the target.

"Designate PC!"

"Up!" Swanny cried.

"Identified!" JJ engaged the target. The turret turned.

"Fire and adjust!"

"On the way!"

The BMP had stopped at the edge of the field and opened its rear doors. Wayland saw Russian troops dismounting, scattering into the long grass. The round struck the stationary vehicle and blew the BMP-3's turret high into the sky, splitting the vehicle wide open and killing every Russian soldier in a withering hail of fragments and shrapnel.

The battlefield looked like the front of a forest fire; a wall of billowing grey smoke, lit from within by the burning ruins of several APCs. Wayland studied his CITV for a fresh target and realized the Russians were retreating. He ordered Swanny to reload with a fresh round of HEAT and then cringed and flinched instinctively as the building in front of the tank erupted in a huge avalanche of debris and dust.

'Crack!'

"Fuck!" Wayland shouted. The whole tank shuddered violently. The ground beneath them shook, coming up through the steel tracks and suspension. Fragments of debris rained down on the tank like heavy hail.

"Identified tank!" J.J cried.

"Fire, fire sabot!"

"On the way!"

The ground immediately in front of the Russian tank erupted so that for several seconds the ridge was veiled in a dense brown curtain of dirt. But there was no fireball to confirm the target's death. Wayland growled his frustration. The tank's thermal sights washed out to a bright green blur, blinded by a thermal smoke screen the enemy tank had fired to conceal its movement. When the image had cleared after several long seconds, the ridge was empty.

The silence after the frantic chaos of combat was crushing. For long seconds the men in the tank held their breath, their eyes searching the distance for fresh targets that never appeared. Wayland wiped sweat from his brow. His hands were trembling like a man in the grips of fever.

"Red, this is One. REDCON status."

"One, this is Two. Zero engaged. REDCON One." Sergeant Rye's tank had been positioned in the eastern streets of the village and had seen no action.

"One, this is Three. Engaged and destroyed three PC's. REDCON One."

"One, Four. Zero engaged. REDCON One," Sergeant McGrath sounded bitterly disappointed that no enemy vehicles had come down the road from Lomza.

There was a moment of collective silence before a new voice cut across the Platoon net.

"Bravo, Red One," Major Browne's voice came loud through Wayland's CVC. "Confirm the enemy are in retreat. Score the first round to us."

*

The Russian withdrawal gave Wayland's tankers a pause in which they could gulp down blood-warm bottled water and mop sweat-drenched brows. The men were exhausted but still tightly strung after the sudden frenetic clamor of combat. Some stared blankly at the steel interior of their tanks while others tried to still trembling hands and slow the frantic drumbeat of their hearts. Wayland popped the turret hatch to ventilate the Abrams with fresh air and hoisted himself up through the cupola. After the confined suffocating environment inside the tank, the afternoon light made him blink to adjust his eyes.

The house his tank was concealed behind had been destroyed. The front wall had collapsed and two internal walls leaned at a precarious angle amidst the sagging remains of the roof. The Abrams was littered with a dusty rubble of broken tiles and shattered glass. Debris lay scattered as far as the road. Amongst the wreckage Wayland saw broken toys, an overturned refrigerator, and a burned bed mattress.

He stared across the sweeping expanse of low farm fields. The smoke screen that had preceded the enemy's attack had been carried away by the breeze. Now just the smoldering ruined APCs littered the battlefield. He peered at the tangled destruction for long minutes and then studied the skyline, inching his gaze along the fringe of trees and ploughed ground beyond which were concealed the Russians. And then, suddenly, he checked and narrowed his eyes.

He had seen a tell-tale tendril of dark diesel exhaust; a smudge that stained the sky for an instant and then dissolved in the air.

He dropped down into the tank and called Major Browne on the Irish company's frequency.

"Sandman Six, this is Red One. Is the drone airborne?" Wayland asked urgently.

"It's just being relaunched now, Red One," the Major, standing on the rooftop of the school building, turned and watched a soldier release the surveillance unit from the palm of his hand. It was like watching a small bird being given flight.

"Get it north," Wayland urged. "I think the Russians are readying for another attack."

"Christ on his cross! Are you sure?"

"No. But I just saw diesel exhaust, or maybe dust from beyond the skyline. They're on the move, and I don't think they're falling back on Lomza. We need to get eyes on what's behind that rise of ground."

"Will do. Standby."

The miniature drone buzzed northwest. Major Browne studied the hand-held monitor as the surveillance unit traversed the battlefield. He counted six destroyed enemy APCs, their blackened carcasses still billowing smoke. Dead Russian soldiers, dismembered body parts, and twisted chunks of shrapnel were scattered throughout the fields. The bodies lay in gruesome heaps amidst patches of burned grass. The carnage showed the battle's progression as the Russians had closed on the village before being repulsed. The fields were rutted with deeply furrowed gouges, churned from the soft ground as the BMP-3s had desperately tried to maneuver away from the menace of the Abrams'. The ragged trail of their tracks revealed the rising chaos of the assault as each vehicle had taken evasive action.

"Okay," Browne was satisfied there was nothing more to learn. "Take the drone north. Let's look at what the Russians are up to."

The operator thumbed the hand-held control and the drone buzzed north, climbing to five thousand feet. Major Browne waited anxiously, wandering to the edge of the rooftop to survey the village below as the minutes ticked by. His eyes settled on the ruined building near the intersection behind which Wayland's Abrams was parked, and then drifted further along the street.

"Major!" one of the drone operators called suddenly.

Browne reached the man in five long strides. He stared in silence at the monitor for several seconds and then lunged for his radio.

"Red One, this is Sandman Six Actual. Russian units beyond the skyline are preparing to attack! Repeat. Russian units preparing for attack."

"Sandman Six Actual, this is Red One. Are they forming to the west again?" Wayland snapped into his CVC radio.

"Aye," Major Browne said. "And there are tanks on the road as well."

"Christ!" Wayland thought quickly, then called up Sergeant Rye's Abrams to the east of the village.

"Two, this is One," Rye had heard the Irish Major's warning. "Abandon your position and move to the intersection to defend the road with Red Four."

Another thick veil of smoke preceded the Russian attack, launched from a dozen points behind the rise. The grenades exploded above the farm fields. The bursts of smoke looked like a sinister fireworks display as each explosion bloomed, then melded together in the air to form an impenetrable drifting curtain. Wayland pulled the turret hatch closed and glued his eyes to the CITV. An afternoon breeze picked up the smoke and carried it slowly towards the village.

The Platoon net was eerily silent.

Wayland spoke into the tense ominous void. "Swanny, load HEAT…"

Chapter 4:

The Russians burst out of the smoke like steel beasts from a nightmare. The BMP-3s attacked across the farm fields flinging up mud and dirt as they charged, firing smoke from their turret-mounted launchers to conceal their advance. At the same time Russian T-90 tanks raced down the main road from Lomza, barreling towards the intersection. It was mid-afternoon and the sun was hidden behind smoke and clouds so that the world seemed unnaturally shadowed with foreboding.

A nest of Irish infantry occupying houses along the northern outskirts of the village fired a hasty volley of FGM-148 Javelin anti-tank missiles, then retreated before the advancing Russian armor. One of the missiles struck the lead tank from a range of less than a thousand yards. The T-90 was slammed by a hammer blow that penetrated the tank's top armor and blew the vehicle apart. It erupted in an explosion of roaring flame, shooting fragments of twisted metal into the nearby trees. The infantry had been placed in the outlying houses to slow any direct advance on the intersection, but no one had expected the Russians to attack in such force, nor so aggressively. The soldiers ghosted back into the village and took up fresh positions, their squad leader shouting at them to keep their heads down. The tanks following the lead vehicle spilled onto the shoulder of the tree-lined road and continued to advance. One of the T-90s fired into the closest house and killed a two-man infantry team, destroying the building in the process. Another Javelin team refused to retreat but instead fired at a T-90 from just a couple of hundred yards. The missile struck the thick angled turret armor of the Russian tank and was deflected into a nearby wall. Russian retribution for the roadside attack was savage. Tanks fired indiscriminately into the building where the men lay hidden, blowing it apart and killing both soldiers.

Hull-down behind a wall at the village intersection, Sergeant McGrath's Abrams opened fire on the advancing Russians. His tank's first shot scored a direct hit on one of the T-90s, striking it broadside as it crashed off the road and into a clump of low bushy trees. The round destroyed the right-side track and the last two road wheels, before tearing through the hull and mutilating the diesel engine, rendering the tank immobile. The crew flung open the hatches and bailed out of the vehicle as it disappeared behind a great billow of smoke. Irish infantry fired on the crewmen as they scampered into a drainage ditch for cover.

McGrath's tank fired again, scoring another direct hit and blowing the paralyzed T-90 to pieces. The smoke and flames from the erupting Russian tank cast a dark oily cloud across the intersection. For a moment the CITV screen inside the Abrams blurred green-white. McGrath cursed the momentary battlefield blindness and clenched his jaw. There were four more T-90s beyond the veil of flames, each of them stalking him. In the tense silence he peered into the smoke and waited. The platoon net erupted in a staccato of chatter.

Rye's Abrams was a hundred yards east of the intersection, parked in the middle of the road, broadside to the Russians. A T-90 appeared from behind an outlying house and dashed across his sights. He barked the order to fire but in the split-second it took to send the round downrange, the Russian had disappeared behind another building. Rye panicked. He had given away his position and now he was petrified with indecision.

He barked a status report across the platoon net, then impulsively ordered his tank forward. The Abrams turned and lunged at the sidewalk, bulldozed through a wooden fence, and then swung in an arc through a vegetable garden. The whine of the great turbine engine drowned out the clamor of the battle. Ahead he saw a clump of trees and a wooden fence. His driver slewed the Abrams sideways. The tank bucked across uneven ground and then, too late, Rye realized his error.

The Russian T-90 had crossed his path and then stopped behind the garage of an adjoining house, cunningly turning its turret back in the direction it had come. Rye had blundered into the trap. He had just a single gut-wrenching heartbeat to recognize his error and to understand the fatal consequences before the Russian tank disappeared behind a violent fiery bloom of muzzle blast.

The Abrams was struck broadside at point-blank range. The round penetrated the tank's ammunition compartment while Rye's loader was in the act of pushing a fresh round into the breach. The open ammunition blast door allowed the explosion to enter the turret and the rest of the tank. The sound of the huge blast shook the air and sent a tremor rumbling through the ground. The impact of the round was so violent that the sixty-ton monster was shunted sideways as it blew apart, killing Rye and his crew instantly.

On the rooftop of the school Major Browne saw the Abrams destroyed and yelled urgent orders to his squad leaders, alerting them that a Russian tank had broken into the network of village streets. A two-man Javelin team hunted the steel beast, dashing through the maze of rubble-strewn buildings while the battle raged around them. When they reached a firing position at the corner of a wooden barn, the T-90 was trundling towards the village intersection. The range was three hundred yards. The crewmen set the Javelin in direct-attack mode and launched.

The missile flew on a feather of flame and smoke straight at the target. The Russian tank swished its tail as it rounded a corner and the anti-tank missile struck flush. A wall of boiling orange flame enveloped the vehicle as it exploded, dislodging the turret from the hull and blowing the sides of the tank apart.

For a moment it seemed the Russian advance along the road had stalled. But there were BMP-3 troop carriers following the T-90s. The vehicles disgorged the infantry they carried a thousand yards north of the village rather than risk the wicked wrath of the Abrams tanks again. Under cover of more smoke and behind broken ground dotted with trees and isolated buildings the troops spilled from the APCs and came towards the village in skirmish order.

The Russian's were met by machine gun fire from two platoons of Irish infantry and a fierce firefight erupted. One group of enemy soldiers dashed diagonally across a field of tall grass towards a woodshed only to discover the small building was defended by three soldiers who cut them down.

From the rooftop of the school building snipers set to work, picking off enemy machine gun teams and killing vehicle commanders in the cupolas of their APCs. One Russian Lieutenant had his brains dashed against the hull of his vehicle from over a thousand yards away by a high-powered sniper rifle. Another was shot in the shoulder and slid down into cover, bloodied and screaming.

A Platoon of Russian infantry advanced down the edge of the road, past the smoldering ruins of the T-90, using the trees for cover. McGrath ordered his gunner to switch from the tank's main gun to the coaxial machine gun in the turret. As the Russians made their next dash forward, the gunner opened fire, flensing leaves and branches from the trees and cutting down the running men. They fell across the blacktop, shattered and broken in dark spreading splashes of their own blood.

The BMP-3s opened fire with their 100mm guns to support the faltering Russian infantry. Rounds rained down on houses, collapsing roofs and demolishing walls. One round set light to a hay barn and the flames crackled into a shower of sparks that ignited spot fires in the long grass.

The Irish Javelin teams returned fire. Two BMPs were struck by anti-tank missiles and destroyed before the remaining vehicles retreated into the woods for safety. Left abandoned, the Russian infantry wavered, then began to edge backwards. The Irish infantry fought on tenaciously, outflanking the enemy from a row of houses on the eastern edge of the village. The Russians were caught in a withering maelstrom of fire and fragment grenades. They broke. A soldier scrambled to his feet and ran into a fusillade of fire intended for the man scampering beside him. He arched his back as the bullets struck him, rising for a second onto his tiptoes, his face wrenched in excruciating pain. He hung like that, seemingly suspended on invisible strings with his arms thrown wide and his mouth hanging open, until two more bullets flung him face forward, dead into the dirt. Another Russian zig-zagged into the path of a thrown grenade and was hurled sideways by the blast, his uniform shredded, his body broken and bleeding. He screamed in gruesome pain and then broke into uncontrollable sobs until he died. Three other fleeing Russians were hit by a swathe of machine gun fire and dropped to the dirt like shot birds, writhing in pain from lower leg wounds. As the Russians retreated, the Irish sprang from their defensive positions and dragged the wounded enemy soldiers back into the village.

On the western edge of Stare Lubiejewo, Wayland and Nossiter's Abrams were left with a single platoon of Irish infantry to fend off a company of BMP-3s that came swarming over the skyline behind a rolling cloud of white smoke. The Russians advanced across a wide front, overlapping the outskirts of the village and threatening the Allied flank. Sergeant Nossiter reversed his tank out of its defensive position between two houses and raced along the street, firing at APC targets on the move. Two enemy armored troop carriers exploded in fireballs just ten seconds apart. The remaining four vehicles in the flank attack slewed to a stop and pumped the air around them with more smoke. Within the dense wall of haze, they flung open their rear doors and the infantry within surged forward. Nossiter could see ghostly shapes moving within the smoke, running ahead of their assault carriers. He ordered his gunner to switch to coax just as a squad of Irish infantry armed with machine guns joined the battle. Bullets plucked at the smoke curtain, punching holes in the dissipating haze and scything down the Russian infantry that, without the cover of smoke, were exposed in the open. They dropped to the ground and returned fire, but quickly realized the futility of their position. Nossiter ordered his tank to advance into the farm fields and the enemy infantry, seeing sixty tons of steel death approaching, turned and fled.

The second wave of APCs skirted the edge of the fields, close to the tree-lined road. Wayland watched the hulking steel shapes drift in and out of the haze. They were advancing in a column, travelling at close to thirty kilometers an hour. It was a suicidal charge.

Wayland waited patiently until the lead vehicle was within eight hundred yards and then snapped an order.

"Designate PC!"

"Up!" Swanny cried.

"Identified!" J.J engaged the target. For the incredible accuracy of the Abrams the range was practically point-blank.

"Fire and adjust!"

"On the way!"

The Abrams rocked on its suspension as the round flew downrange. The lead BMP-3 took the hit flush on the hull and was flung into the air by the impact. It blew upwards and then blew apart. The shattering explosion hurled the turret over the top of a nearby tree and ripped the vehicle to pieces.

"Target!" J.J announced.

Ten seconds later the Abrams fired again, destroying a second Russian armored carrier and the men inside. But the Russians were determined to drive home their attack. Machine gun fire pinged against the Abrams armored hull from a third charging BMP-3.

The Russian driver was a cunning veteran. He zig-zagged his vehicle across the open ground and then crashed through trees and veered across the road.

"Shit!" Wayland shouted. "Driver, hold your left and back up fast. Put me on the main road."

The driver wrenched the throttle handle and the Abrams surged backwards, crushing a chicken coop, then slewing through a plot of lemon trees. Wayland reached for a hand-hold as the tank bucked and rocked, then stabilized in the middle of the dual carriageway, fifty yards south of the intersection.

Wayland saw the BMP-3 directly ahead through his CITV. "Designate PC!"

"Identified!" J.J. engaged the target. When he thumbed the laser button, the range display on his sight showed two hundred meters.

"Fire and adjust!" Wayland barked.

"On the way!" J.J. crushed the trigger.

The HEAT round struck the BMP-3 on the turret and the vehicle erupted in an explosion of flames. The percussion of the huge blast blew out the windows of a nearby house and fragments of burning debris set the roof on fire.

Wayland checked the BMS. The Russians were withdrawing behind another heavy veil of smoke. Wayland punched open the hatch and heaved himself up through the cupola like a deep-sea diver coming to the surface for air. He felt physically and mentally exhausted. He peered down the road, past Sergeant McGrath's tank, and stared with a kind of macabre fascination at the scene of unholy devastation. His hands shook and a nerve in his leg trembled uncontrollably. A wave of nausea and then relief washed over him.

They had survived.

They had held the village.

For now…

*

In the absence of artillery support, the Russians retreated behind the skyline and used their T-90s to bombard the village, firing HE-FRAG rounds from the dead ground three kilometers north of the intersection.

High Explosive-Fragmentation munitions were created for use against 'soft' targets such as military trucks and troops in light cover, and were designed to kill by exploding a lethal hail of shrapnel fragments across the battle zone.

"Take cover!" Major Browne shouted over the Irish company's radio net.

The first Russian round landed in a field to the east of the technical school, flensing the leaves from trees but doing no real damage. A second round landed in the field northeast of the intersection where the Russian infantry had, less than an hour before, been repulsed by two platoons of Irish infantry. The explosion ripped up a ten-yard wide crater of earth but killed no one. The men in the field were already dead.

The third round struck a home at the eastern end of the village, crashing through the roof and flattening the building. An elderly civilian died in the blast. The fourth Russian round destroyed a shed filled with farm equipment on the western side of the village when it tore through the rafters of the building, killing an Irish sniper and wounding two others who had to be dragged from the burning wreckage.

"We've got injuries, sir!" the company radio operator told Major Browne. "One man killed and a couple seriously injured."

"Where?"

"Farm shed, west side."

Major Browne went to the edge of the school building's rooftop and trained his binoculars west to where a column of brown smoke rose into the afternoon sky. "What about the prisoners?"

"They're downstairs. The doc is patching them up."

"How long before they can be interrogated?"

"Fifteen minutes."

The prisoners were three soldiers who had suffered leg wounds in the Russian infantry attack across the northeastern field and had been captured by the Irish defenders as their comrades had fled the battle. Now they were on the ground floor of the school building in a locked and guarded room being attended to by medical staff. Two of the Russians were expected to survive their injuries.

Browne grunted. "I'll be back." He left Captain O'Malley in command on the rooftop and went downstairs, then out through the ground floor doors.

The Russian bombardment continued. Rounds screamed down on the village at random intervals. One explosion flattened a row of small iron-roofed garden sheds near a sports field. The torrent of shrapnel from the explosion killed another infantryman, decapitating him. For long seconds after his death the body still spasmed and twitched in a spreading pool of dark red blood.

Another round landed in the carpark of the school, destroying several abandoned cars and setting two of them alight.

Through the mayhem and chaos, Major Browne, magnificently casual, strode across the intersection like a man on pleasant Sunday afternoon stroll. He reached Wayland's Abrams and rapped his knuckles politely on the steel hull. Wayland pushed open the hatch and hung his head out of the turret.

"Are you mad, Major?" Wayland gasped his incredulity.

"Yes. Probably," the Irish officer smiled disarmingly. "But I thought you might like to know that the prisoners we captured are ready to be interrogated, so they are. Would you be wanting to listen in to what they have to say for themselves?"

*

The three Russian prisoners were lying on stretchers in the corner of a school janitor's room beside a shelf of buckets and cloth rags. Their wounds had been bandaged but pain-killers had been withheld until the interrogation was completed. Major Browne and Wayland stood in the threshold of the room and studied the soldiers. One wore three Sergeant stripes on his sleeve. The other two men were Privates. The Sergeant had a shaved head and tattooed arms. He looked stern and grizzled, but his face was shiny with sweat, his flesh doughy white with pain.

The other two prisoners looked like boys. They were thin and frightened. One had a face scarred with acne, his pale eyes nervous. He lay on his back, whimpering, his lower left leg swollen by a thick covering of bandages.

"Everyone outside," Major Browne said brusquely to the medical staff. When the room was clear, he ushered a

Corporal through the door who spoke Russian. The soldier stood against the far wall and tried to make himself invisible.

Wayland and Major Browne exchanged glances. Then the Russian Sergeant broke into a stream of rapid speech. His voice was coarse and throaty; the sound of a heavy smoker.

"What did he say?" the Major demanded.

"He said they are prisoners of war and are protected under the Geneva Convention."

Major Browne smiled grimly and his eyes turned hard. "Tell the man that we have tended to his injuries, but we cannot guarantee he still will not die of his wounds…"

Wayland kept his face impassive but behind his eyes he recoiled. He had not glimpsed the dark side of the Irish officer's personality. He wondered what kind of man the amiable good-natured façade was hiding.

The soldier translated and there was a pause. The Russian spoke again, this time warily.

"He said you are threatening him, sir."

"Quite right," Major Browne's voice was humorless. "I'm making it clear that our own injured soldiers get priority medical attention. Unless these men can tell me something of value, they will receive further medical aid only when our own troops have been attended to… and only if we have medical supplies left to administer."

The translation took time to relay the message and then the Russian and the translator broke into a short flurry of back and forth speech.

"What's he saying?" Major Browne cut in.

"He asked what you wanted to know," the translator explained. "I told him we wanted details of the enemy force facing us. He said he was under no obligation to reveal that information and I remined him that if he didn't, we couldn't guarantee any of them would survive their injuries."

"And…?"

"He's thinking about it, sir."

Major Browne smiled coldly. The Russian Sergeant returned the stare as the two men matched wills.

It was the Major who broke first. He went out through the door for a moment and when he returned he was holding a grenade. "Tell the prisoner he has ten seconds to start talking," Browne's voice was as savage as the blade of a dagger. His eyes had turned dark and predatory. The translator's face paled and there was urgency and real alarm in his tone as he spat the words out in faltering Russian.

The burly sergeant looked incredulous, then defiant – then uncertain. He licked his lips and his head turned to regard the two Privates on the stretchers beside him. His shoulders slumped and when he spoke again Major Browne didn't need a translation to understand the Russian had capitulated.

"Ask him who is in command of the enemy force in front of us."

"He says the commander is Lieutenant Colonel Pugacheva, a great and celebrated hero of the Army," the translator interpreted.

Wayland and Major Browne exchanged glances. "Ever heard of him?"

"No," Wayland shook his head.

Major Browne glanced back to the translator. "Ask him the size of the force in front of us."

The Russian spoke for several minutes and then lapsed into panting silence. He wrenched his face in agony and clutched at his bandaged leg.

"He says we are facing a Battalion Tactical Group made up of a motorized rifle battalion in BMP-3s with two companies of T-90 tanks in support. But he says the rest of the Russian Army will begin arriving tomorrow morning, or maybe tonight, including artillery, thousands of infantry and many more tanks."

Major Browne said nothing. He studied the Russian Sergeant's expression and then abruptly turned on his heel and left the room. Wayland and the translator filed through the door behind him.

Outside in the hallway, the Irish Major looked deep in thought. "Well, Lieutenant? Do you think he's lying?"

"I don't think so," Wayland said. "I don't see the point. We know the Russian Army is concentrated on Lomza. And we know they could reach here in a matter of hours. We know they're making a push for Warsaw. The only thing in dispute is the size of the force we're currently facing. But if they had more tanks and BMPs, or if they had a battery of heavy artillery, they would have used them against us before now. It all seems to check out."

"Yes," Major Browne agreed. "Not that any of the information helps us."

"No. We are where we were fifteen minutes ago – in the fight for our lives to hold the village against everything the Russians can throw against us."

Chapter 5:

Wayland stood in the courtyard of the school building and stared at the ruins of the village. A dozen houses were on fire and just as many more had been reduced to rubble. In the fields to the north, bodies lay crumpled in the dirt amidst the burned out wreckage of Russian BMP-3s. Closer, he saw the T-90 that had been destroyed by the Irish Javelin team, the turret askew, the barrel bent, the steel hull of the ruined tank charred black.

And near to it was Sergeant Rye's destroyed Abrams.

Wayland had only known the Sergeant and his crew for just a few hours, yet he felt profoundly anguished by their loss. After the Battle of Jekabpils in Lithuania he had wondered if he had lost his nerve. He had left that battlefield numbed and senseless; unable to feel anything other than relief and exhaustion. Now he felt renewed determination, sharpened by the poignancy of his grief. It was as if a blade, dulled and blunted, had been reforged in the flames of this tragedy. For over twenty years he had trained for war. Fighting was all he knew – and it was with a sense of guilty relief that he realized he still had a purpose and a point to prove.

He looked up at the clouds. They were building across the horizon, brooding with the promise of more rain. Then he looked north. The skyline was empty. The Russians would be tending to their casualties and assessing their losses. They had ceased firing on the village for the moment and the air was ominously still.

Wayland set out for his tank, stepping through dust and rubble that lay strewn across the blacktop. A middle-aged woman, her head wrapped in a floral scarf, was on her knees in front of a small house, tending to her ruined garden that had been trampled during the frantic fighting. Wayland gaped with incredulity, but said nothing. Flies buzzed and carrion birds circled in the sky overhead.

Then, from the south, he heard the distant whine of heavy engines and the clatter of steel tracks. He turned and stared.

The road from Warsaw suddenly filled with a column of Abrams tanks.

Captain Kohn and the rest of 'C' Company had arrived.

*

The lead Platoon of Abrams' stopped in the middle of the road. The rest of the column filed into the parking lot in front of the hotel that stood several hundred yards short of the intersection. There were ten tanks in total as well as several company support vehicles, including an M113A3 APC Medic track, and an M106A3 mortar track. At the tail of the column followed an M1083 A1 cargo truck filled with company supplies and the giant M88A2 Hercules Recovery Vehicle – one of the largest ARV's used by US Armed Forces. There was no room for either vehicle in the parking lot. Their drivers beached them on the opposite side of the road under a stand of trees.

Captain Kohn climbed down from his Abrams and strode towards Wayland, his steps purposeful, his expression agitated.

"You look like hell, Wayland."

"It's been a hard day's work, sir. We've fought off two determined Russian attacks and destroyed a number of enemy APCs and tanks. We also lost an Abrams. Sergeant Rye's vehicle was destroyed near the intersection."

Captain Kohn was too restless to pay attention. His eyes seemed to be everywhere at once. "Don't tell me, Lieutenant. Show me!"

He strode towards the intersection with Wayland at his side. Pounding footsteps behind them announced the arrival of XO, Lieutenant Grimmet. Together the three men toured the village with Wayland describing details of the Russian attacks and the disposition of the Irish infantry.

"Do you think the Russians will attack again?" the Captain was excited by the prospect of action and struggling to keep his eagerness from showing.

"The Irish captured three enemy prisoners during the last wave of attacks. According to them, the entire Russian Army will be behind that low rise you can see in the distance by tomorrow morning."

"You believe him, Wayland?"

"I've no reason not to, Captain."

Kohn grunted. He kept walking north, past the destroyed T-90 in the middle of the blacktop until he was beyond the last few houses that marked the northern outskirts of the village, blithely ignorant of the threat that enemy snipers represented. For a long moment he stared into the distance.

"Wayland? How many tanks and APCs did the prisoner say the Russians had on the battlefield at the moment?"

"Two T-90 companies and a battalion of BMP-3s with infantry, sir. They're behind that gentle rise of land," he pointed through the trees that lined the road. "You can still see the tracks the BMP-3s left when they launched their first assault against the western edge of the village."

Kohn peered. The skyline crouched beneath a towering bank of storm clouds, cast in gloomy shadow. Nothing moved.

"Drones?"

"The Irish have been operating a couple of miniature battlefield units, sir. The rise of ground is about the limit of their range."

Kohn nodded. "And where is Major Browne?"

"His command post is in a school building near the intersection."

"Very well," Kohn turned on his heel and strode back towards the village. "Please tell the Major that I will be holding a briefing at that hotel where our company is assembled…," he glanced at his watch, "…in twenty minutes time. I would be grateful if he could join us."

Wayland nodded. Kohn glanced over his shoulder at Lieutenant Grimmet. "XO, let's get the tanks into position. I want White Platoon to the west of the main road and Blue Platoon concentrated around the intersection," he pointed as he spoke. "You will attach your tank to Red Platoon to replace Wayland's lost vehicle."

"Sir," Grimmet hesitated. "It's going to take more than twenty minutes to get them in position and hull down behind defensive cover…"

"No defensive cover for now. Just get them in place. Wayland, I want your Platoon oriented to the east."

"Sir?"

"You heard me, Lieutenant."

Wayland drew a breath and put patience into his voice. "I heard you, Captain, but the Russians can't attack the village from the east. That flank is protected by miles of dense forest."

Kohn stopped in mid-stride and glared at Wayland irritably. His face flushed with temper. "Are you refusing to obey an order, Lieutenant?"

"No, sir," Wayland said stiffly. "I'm merely pointing out that the order you're giving wastes the firepower of my three tanks."

Lieutenant Grimmet's face flushed crimson with acute embarrassment. Captain Kohn licked his lips. "What did you say, Lieutenant?" His voice was filled with obscene loathing.

Wayland stood his ground. Captain Kohn clenched his jaw and his eyes turned dark. "You have your orders, Lieutenant Wayland. I expect you to obey them."

*

The Platoon leaders, Kohn and Grimmet, all gathered at the hotel and were led to a window table that offered a panoramic view across miles of featureless farmland.

A middle-aged woman fussed around the edges of the meeting. The hotel was not open, but the owners had refused to evacuate to Warsaw. The woman was short and squat with an unlovely face, an apron around her waist, and a tangle of grey hair atop her head, held in place by pins and clips.

The hotel dining room had been decorated in the style of a Bavarian hunting lodge. The walls were dark wood panelling, covered with framed hunting prints and deer heads. The wooden floors were covered in animal furs. Above the unlit fireplace hung an oil painting of the Polish countryside, and from the low wooden beamed ceiling dangled chandeliers.

The hotel was dark, even in daylight. The power had been cut to the village so there were candles on the table beside a bottle of wine and several glasses. The wine remained unopened.

Major Browne and Captain O'Malley arrived and were greeted by Captain Kohn like long-lost relatives. Kohn was magnanimous in his praise for the Irish infantry's resolute defense of the village and in turn the Irish officer graciously pointed out the valiant heroics of Wayland's tank platoon. The polite flattery dispensed with, Captain Kohn brusquely called the meeting to order.

"Gentlemen, I believe we have been presented with an opportunity," he began optimistically as the chatter around the table stilled. "I think the Russians have made a mistake – one we can exploit for a decisive victory."

Across the table Wayland and Major Browne exchanged suspicious glances. The Major shifted uncomfortably in his seat.

"An opportunity, you say, Captain Kohn?"

"Yes," Kohn answered. Lieutenant Grimmet handed him satellite images of the terrain surrounding Stare Lubiejewo. As intelligence the photos were useless – almost twenty-four hours old. But they did detail the landscape beyond the low rise. Kohn laid them out on the table. "The land past the skyline crest is a flat, sunken basin," he described the area with his hand like a magician conjuring a spell. "It's bisected by the road and fringed to the north and west by a dense barrier of forest." Each man seated at the table craned forward to study the images. "In other words… it's a trap. The Russians have positioned themselves for an attack on the village, but they haven't considered the possibility they might be the ones pushed onto the defensive. And if a successful attack against them was launched, they would be caught in this basin, with their only means of retreat back along the road – back towards Lomza."

For a long moment frowns and dark glances of alarm were passed discreetly around the table. Major Browne cleared his throat. "Would you be thinking about attacking the Russians then, Captain?"

"Yes."

"Sir, you can't be serious," Wayland looked appalled.

Kohn turned on Wayland his eyes hostile and bulging. "You have something to say, Lieutenant?"

"Yes, sir," Wayland rose to his feet. "Why are we considering an attack? We have orders to defend the village. The enemy must come to us across open ground. Our troops and tanks are in good positions. It makes no sense."

"You're afraid of meeting the enemy head on," Kohn sneered, and Wayland saw the other Platoon Leaders smile at the jibe. "We are considering the merit of an attack because it's the best form of defense, and because the secret of war is to do the things your enemy is least prepared for. According to your report from Major Browne's prisoners – the enemy has a couple of tank companies and a battalion of BMPs."

"It's considerably less than that, now," Wayland spoke. All eyes turned to him. "After their two attacks against the village so far today, we've destroyed probably a full company of personnel carriers and several T-90s."

Kohn arched his eyebrows. The woman proprietor scuttled across the room carrying a platter of Rolada z kurczakiem i pieczarkami and set it at the edge of the table. They were mushroom-stuffed chicken roulade appetizers in an egg-cheese coating made with thin chicken breast slices topped with fried mushrooms and onions, then rolled up and baked in an egg-cheese batter.

The woman looked belligerently at Captain Kohn and wiped her hands on her apron. Her brows were beetling, her eyes rheumy. She spoke in a flurry of rapid Polish and then abruptly turned on her heel and scuttled away.

Kohn looked bewildered. Major Browne made a sympathetic grimace. "She says," he interpreted, "that this is the best she can do, so you can eat it or starve. And she also wanted to know when will the bloody Russians stop blowing up the village?"

Kohn blinked, then turned on Wayland, picking up the thread of the last comment.

"Well your information just makes the case for an attack even more compelling."

"No, sir. It doesn't."

"Why?"

"Because we hurt the Russians by doing exactly what we were ordered to do – defending the village and letting them expose themselves in the open. It's a strategy that has so far proven successful," the jibe went home, provoking nods of agreement from the Irish Major and his Captain.

Kohn snapped at Wayland. "That doesn't diminish the tactical soundness of compounding those enemy losses with an attack that would sweep them off the field."

"What you are proposing, sir," Wayland sensed he had overstepped the mark but it was too late now, "is an attack against an enemy of unknown size, in unknown positions behind rise of ground that conceals their movements. They could have been reinforced by fresh units from Lomza. Or they could have tanks concealed in that wall of woods. We won't know what we're facing until we crest the skyline, leaving us exposed, disoriented by unfamiliar terrain, and unsure where the enemy are positioned."

Kohn huffed with contempt. "Well, given your lack of enthusiasm for bold action, you will be pleased to know, Lieutenant Wayland, that your Platoon will not be part of the main assault."

Wayland ignored the information. "So you've made up your mind, sir? You're going to attack the Russians?"

"Yes, damn it," Kohn let his hostility show. "Yes, we are. And I want no more comments from you. Your objections have been noted, Lieutenant Wayland, and I will be certain to highlight your protest when I file my report about your performance to Battalion command." It was a threat, but not one Wayland cared about. Kohn clawed his hands through his hair, struggling to keep his temper in check. Wayland sat down and stared contemplatively out through the window.

Captain Kohn fetched salt and pepper shakers, wine bottles and glasses and arranged them on the tabletop, using the surface and condiments for a makeshift sand-table briefing.

"Now," he drew a deep breath to calm his umbrage, "This is how we're going to advance on the enemy."

Using a line of salt to delineate the main road and a handful of wine glasses to represent the Company's tanks, Kohn took the men around the table step-by-step through the assault.

"Red Platoon will stay east of the road in reserve while I lead White and Blue Platoons west of the village, across the farm fields. When we reach the rise, the two Platoons will fan out, with White Platoon hooking further west to drive the Russians towards the road. Once we have the enemy in disarray, Blue Platoon will crest the rise, maximizing their confusion. Wayland's Platoon will close the trap, preventing the retreating enemy from using the road to escape." It sounded remarkably simple. "Any questions?"

Wayland met Captain Kohn's eyes. He spoke with stiff formality. "Are we expecting reinforcements from Warsaw to help defend the village, sir?"

"What?"

"Are we expecting reinforcements, sir?"

"Yes."

"When?"

"Soon."

"What units will be sent to support us?" Wayland persisted earnestly.

"I don't know, Lieutenant."

"But reinforcements are coming?"

"God damn it, man. Yes!" In truth he did not know when the beleaguered defenders holding the village would be reinforced, or even if they would be reinforced. The focus of all his attention was on launching his surprise attack. "Command knows the Russian Army will fall upon this place by tomorrow morning. We'll have support before then." He hammered the table with his fist and then glared around the room one last time, daring anyone else to challenge him. "Are there any questions about the attack? No? Good. Brief your men. We move out in one hour."

*

The Abrams' of White and Blue platoon advanced from the western outskirts of the village, setting out across the farm fields towards the skyline rise two kilometers away. They passed the burned out remains of the Russian APCs, each commander eyeing the distant ridge warily. They were formed line abreast, with Kohn's command tank in the center of the line between the two Platoons. On the eastern flank, Wayland gave curt orders across the Red Platoon net. Before the tanks rolled north along the road to support the attack, Major Browne strode across to Wayland's tank.

"This is a bloody silly thing to do, so it is."

"Yes." There was nothing more to say.

The Irish Major looked away into the distance and when he turned back, he seemed suddenly saddened. "You are unfortunate in your commanding officer."

"Yes."

Browne shrugged and his expression became wan. "If it makes you feel any better, all Armies have fools in command."

Red Platoon turned north, following the main road past the burned wreckage of the Russian T-90, with Nossiter's tank in the lead. Through the trees that lined the side of the road Wayland watched the rest of the company advance across the fields. Despite his foreboding, it was a heroic, stirring spectacle; the Abrams' dashing across the open plain at high speed, trailing thrown dust and dirt in their wake. Wayland fervently prayed the enemy would not notice the attack, prayed that they would crest the skyline unobserved.

When the charging Abrams' were half way across the fields, Captain Kohn peered through the commander's forward periscope and saw two Russian BMP-3s silhouetted against the brooding sky. The enemy vehicles both fired their 100mm guns. One round landed short of the charging Abrams' and threw up a thick veil of dirt. The second round landed long, destroying a hedgerow.

"All tanks, this is Black Six. Enemy in sight on the ridge. Engage at will!"

The Russians fired smoke, and behind swirling brown clouds retreated from view, chased away by a shot from Kohn's gunner that missed.

"Advance at full speed!" Kohn's voice across the Company net was loud and adrenalin infused. "They're retreating! White Platoon, break west now and encircle. Blue Platoon, get to the skyline!"

Wayland watched the Abrams' close on the skyline with a rising sense of apprehension. He had heard the retort of the Russian guns and could see the American tanks closing at high speed. The Russian smoke screen had begun to dissipate as the two Platoons of charging tanks angled up the gentle slope and then finally reached the crest.

Perhaps Kohn had been right, Wayland prayed. If the Abrams' could strike with the element of surprise, they could catch the Russians disorganized. Maybe the alert would be raised too late. Perhaps the enemy would get off a couple of long-range shots that would do little damage before the Abrams fell upon them like wolves amongst a flock of sheep.

Perhaps…

It seemed to Wayland, observing from the distant road and with his view obscured by trees, that two of the Abrams tanks reached the crest of the rise and stopped to fire smoke. He frowned – and then the wicked 'crack!' of heavy guns firing echoed on the air.

The two Abrams were engulfed in black haze. Both vehicles took direct hits. One tank was struck front-on. The round smashed the left track, immobilizing the vehicle. The second Abrams took a turret hit as the main gun was traversing. The sabot round went straight through the armor, killing everyone inside the vehicle. It ground to a halt and a column of black smoke poured into the sky.

"Fuck!" Captain Kohn's tank was beside the Abrams that had taken the front hit. He saw the vehicle disappear behind an eruption of smoke and heard the wicked retort of the round striking. He saw new enemy tanks appear on the far side of the pan, emerging from within a palisade of dense woods.

Kohn's tank swooped over the crest and rolled down the reverse slope. At least a dozen BMP-3s were scattered across the depression. His gunner opened fire, killing two of the troop carriers in quick succession.

But then the Russian tanks fired again. Two shots struck Kohn's vehicle. The sound inside the steel beast was the deafening toll of a huge bell. The first round seemed to shunt the tank backwards, clanging off the front hull. The second round struck the turret. The round was defeated by the tank's composite armor, but the wicked impact knocked Kohn from his command seat like a man thrown from a bucking horse. He cracked his head against a steel edge and blood gushed into his eyes. For a moment he teetered, disoriented and swaying, then collapsed unconscious.

Wayland watched the two Abrams' struck on the crest of the rise and waited for the smoke to clear; waited for them to plunge down the far side of the slope. Neither tank moved. Then he saw Kohn's command vehicle hit by two rounds just as it descended the slope and slid out of slight. The Abrams emerged from the smoke and flames seemingly undamaged, but somehow suddenly sluggish.

"Christ!" he spat. The Russians had sent the BMP-3s to the crest to lure the Americans into a carefully laid trap! He pounced onto the Company net, his voice urgent. "Black Six,

Red One. Get out of there! The Russians are waiting for you. Get out of there!"

There was no direct reply from Kohn's tank but the company net suddenly filled with a garble of confused voices, some shouting in alarm, others in rising panic. It was chaos.

Wayland reacted impulsively. "Red One to Red Platoon. Follow me and battle carry sabot. We're going to join the fight!"

*

The BMP-3s fled across the flat basin, zig-zagging to throw off the fire of the Abrams' that hunted them. But it was not the mad panicked mayhem of a rout; it was the cunning lure of a clever enemy. For behind the armored troop carriers, bristling at the edge of the woods, were a Company of T-90 main battle tanks, arrayed like game hunters waiting for the prey to be herded onto their guns.

On command, the BMP-3s swung east and west, clearing the field of fire for their waiting tanks. The guns flashed huge mushrooming fireballs as each T-90 fired and rocked back on its suspension.

Only the composite armor of the Abrams' saved the two Platoons from slaughter.

One Abrams was struck a glancing blow on the turret and returned fire, hitting a Russian tank as it reversed and turned, presenting itself broadside for just a few seconds. The tank heaved upwards, turned into flame and oily black smoke. The explosion rumbled then crashed like thunder across the brooding sky. The flash of the explosion lasted just a few seconds, and then the smoke began to boil from sprung hatches.

Three other Abrams took hits. Two deflected harmlessly, but the third tank was struck on the right side, destroying two roadwheels and snapping the caterpillar track. The great band of huge steel links unspooled and the tank ground to a standstill, stranded in the open. The crew bailed out of the vehicle but were cut down by machine gun fire from a BMP-3. The four men died face-down in the dirt, one of them clutching at his stomach and retching blood.

"Black Six Actual is down! Black Six Actual is down," the gunner in Captain Kohn's tank screamed across the radio. Wayland heard the panicked voice and searched the battlefield. He saw Kohn's tank at the bottom of the slope, surrounded by drifting smoke. The other tanks in the attack were strung out in the middle of the pan.

"Fall back!" someone shouted across the Company net. The tanks leading the charge suddenly faltered, slowed, then began to swerve away from the waiting Russians.

"Oh, Christ!" Wayland groaned. At any moment the battlefield was going to turn into a shambles. "Red Platoon, line abreast," Wayland ordered the tanks to change out of a column. "Concentrate your fire on the T-90s at the fringe of the woods. Keep the bastards under pressure."

The four tanks of Red Platoon opened fire, charging diagonally across the plain. BMP-3s swerved around them and the battlefield became confused behind swirling dust and a maelstrom of noise. The lead Abrams fired smoke to conceal their retreat, adding to the confusion.

"Fall back! Fall back!" Wayland's voice dominated the company net. "Get behind the rise."

Lieutenant Grimmet stared at the battlefield through his CITV with eyes that were red-rimmed and swollen. The chaos appalled him. He could not remember ever feeling so elated, terrified or disoriented. He had expected a battle to be an orderly affair where the enemy dutifully fired a few panicked shots and then fled in turmoil. But this was a nightmare of noise and dust and smoke, and a radio net filled with screams of anguish and panic.

"Open fire!" Wayland barked. The four Abrams of Red Platoon made a suicidal charge, drawing spiteful revenge from the Russians who saw their trap being sprung at the very moment it was ready to close. Sergeant Nossiter's tank took a glancing hit on the turret that sent a shudder through the steel beast but did not slow it. A moment later it took a second hit that penetrated the flimsy tail armor as the tank swerved around a destroyed BMP-3. The men inside the Abrams never saw death coming. They surged into a wall of black boiling smoke and never emerged. The round tore the tank open, smashed through the engine, and went on to kill every man inside. When the smoke around the vehicle cleared, the destroyed Abrams was sagging heavily to one side, the barrel limp against the ground and the hull blackened.

Suddenly it became a race. The Russian tanks surged from their positions along the perimeter of the woods and charged across the pan. The Abrams were reversing, still firing, trying desperately to reach the crest of the rise and the safety of the farm fields beyond. Wayland saw a T-90 flash across his sights and barked the order to fire.

"Designate tank!"

"Up!" Swanny shouted.

"Identified!" JJ engaged the target. The range was less than five hundred yards.

"Fire and adjust!"

"On the way!"

The Abrams was thrown back on its suspension by the savage recoil. The T-90 disappeared behind a blinding flash of fire. It had been struck broadside. The round hit precisely at the join between the turret and the hull. Smoke boiled up from the stricken tank, then began venting through the barrel. A split-second later the vehicle erupted like a volcano, shooting a fierce jet of flame sixty feet into the air through the top of the turret as the main gun's ammunition cooked off. The phenomenon lasted just a few seconds, and when the fire had died down the tank was black and broken.

"Target!" JJ confirmed. "Man, did you see that fuckin' thing blowtorch?"

Wayland hadn't. He was already searching for fresh targets.

Now there were men on the battlefield, some running from damaged tanks, others staggering, confused and wounded.

They drifted in and out of the smoke, their faces ghastly with pain and fear. A Russian tanker staggered away from a disabled vehicle only to be crushed under the tracks of a BMP-3. Another man – an American – stood clutching at the severed stump of his arm, staggering in the swirling dust. His face was a rictus of agony. He teetered and then fell to his knees as his blood soaked the dry grass.

"Designate tank!" Wayland called another target. The T-90 drifted in and out of swirling smoke.

"Up!" Swanny shouted as another round of sabot was heaved into the breech.

"I've got no shot!" J.J snapped. The Abrams swerved around a crumpled dead body, swishing its tail and kicking up dust. The gunner's view cleared.

"Identified!"

"Fire and adjust!"

"On the way!"

The shot struck the T-90 on the hull, but when the flash of the blast and the boiling smoke drifted away the tank seemed undamaged. Wayland saw the enemy vehicle turning its turret towards him.

"Re-engage!"

"Up!"

"Fire and kill the bastard!"

"On the way!" J.J cried as once again the Abrams sagged on its suspension from the wicked recoil. The Russian tank seemed to fire at the same time. Wayland heard the mighty 'clang!' of a round striking the Abrams' front armor. He ducked and flinched instinctively. When he looked out his periscope again, the Russian tank was enveloped in black smoke.

The Red Platoon's charge had bought time for the remaining Abrams' of Blue and White Platoon to retreat beyond the rise and into the protection of the Irish infantry's Javelin teams. Wayland realized his three tanks were the last survivors of the disastrous attack. He ordered them to break off and scramble to safety.

They withdrew in reverse, still firing while keeping their thick frontal armor facing the enemy. Lieutenant Grimmet's tank took a hit from a T-90 as it reached the safety of the rise. The Russian fired just as the lower hull of Grimmet's Abrams became exposed. For a spilt-second the vehicle teetered at the crest, its barrel swinging upwards as it began to reverse down the slope. The Russian round ripped through the weak underbelly of the Abrams and exploded inside the hull. Remarkably the tank remained intact, but the slaughter caused within the confines of the Abrams was apocalyptic. Smoke billowed from blown hatches as Grimmet and his crew burned.

Wayland watched, ashen-faced, as the XO's tank erupted in a flash of fire and then a towering column of black smoke.

"Christ!"

The attack had been an abject disaster, and now there would be only an ignominious retreat to mark the sacrifice of the dead and dying.

Chapter 6:

Even before the beleaguered remnants of the American attack straggled back to the safety of the village, the Russians launched a counter attack. They came in two determined waves; a column of T-90s trundling down the road and another swarm of BMP-3s across the open fields. This time the enemy troop carriers had circled further to the west. When they appeared suddenly on the horizon, they were threatening to cut off the road from Ostrow Mazowiecka, jeopardizing to sever the allied line of retreat to Warsaw.

The first Wayland knew of the Russian encircling maneuver was when the middle-aged proprietor from the hotel came running, red-faced, towards the intersection. Exhausted and sweating she blurted in a staccato of Polish that she had seen dust on the horizon from an upstairs room, and then a Russian tank.

Major Browne sent two infantrymen to investigate. They came back a minute later to confirm the report. But the Russian vehicles were not tanks. They were a company of BMP-3s driving to intersect the road to Ostrow Mazowiecka.

"The bastards are trying to get around behind us," Major Browne looked up at Wayland, leaning out from his turret cupola.

"Sounds like they already have," Wayland said grimly. His tank was low on sabot ammunition and fuel, but he had HEAT rounds. It took Wayland only a few seconds to understand the implications of the danger; there was no decision to be made. He would take his tank south towards the enemy, hoping he could intercept the Russians before they could secure the road. He spoke to Sergeant McGrath on the Platoon net. The Sergeant's tank was parked on the shoulder of the road, the hatches open to ventilate the interior, the huge turbine engine still running. "Four, this is One. Follow me. We've got another fight to win."

Wayland and McGrath were the only two surviving tanks of Red Platoon. Major Browne hastily pulled twenty men he could ill-afford to lose from the western end of the village.

They clambered onto the hulls of the two Abrams and clung on precariously as the vehicles raced to intersect the Russians.

Wayland urged his driver to hurry. There was little time. The road was flat, lined with trees on both sides. Wayland stood upright in the turret, scanning the road ahead. The tree-lined blacktop turned every new corner into a blind risk, but he had no choice. He had no doubt the Russian infantry would be armed with RPGs and that he was most likely charging towards disaster.

As had happened before during his fighting career, Wayland began to feel the familiar sense of time slowing down, and his mind became detached. He began to recognize irrelevant features on the landscape; it seemed as if the world were moving around him with he at its center. He noticed the color of the leaves on each tree, the coarseness of the blacktop, the broken shards of glass and pieces of litter along the gravel verge as the tank raced by. He could hear nothing over the vast whine of the Abrams' turbine engine, but his instincts became heightened, and with it a witch's brew of emotions bubbled to the surface. He felt the first stirring of elation and anticipation, and also the familiar sense of fear.

Then suddenly the two Abrams rounded a sweeping bend and ran head-long into the Russian BMP-3s, five hundred yards down the road. Four vehicles were parked across the blacktop with the rest of the company spread out into nearby fields. Infantry were spilling out of the back of each APC and forming up behind soft cover. Wayland saw an officer waving his arm frantically and shouting at his troops. One of the BMP-3s fired its main gun. The round struck McGrath's hull front-on and for a moment the Abrams was shrouded in smoke. It burst through the brown boiling haze undamaged.

Far, far away, muted by distance and the whine of the Abrams' engines, Wayland heard the 'crump!' of multiple explosions and understood the troops and tanks back at the intersection were engaging the T-90s. But that was not his fight. All he could do was deal with the danger directly ahead of him as quickly and as savagely as he could. The fight for the intersection was another man's war for now.

Wayland dropped down into the turret and sealed the hatch. The Abrams slewed to a momentary halt, and the Irish infantry riding on the backs of the tanks scrambled into roadside cover. Some men flung themselves down behind trees. Others dived into the shallow drainage ditch that edged the road.

"Four, One. Charge the bastards. Hit 'em hard. Engage at will." Wayland ordered.

The two tanks surged forward, firing as they closed the range. Through his CITV Wayland could see Russian troops crouched behind the steel cover of their APCs. They were shooting at the Irish infantry. Wayland ordered JJ to fire on the four enemy vehicles blocking the road. Two of the BMP-3s exploded in quick succession, blown apart by a hammer blow of HEAT rounds that destroyed the APCs and killed a handful of the infantrymen in close proximity. Most of the Russian soldiers were immolated in the searing fireballs that engulfed the vehicles. Some were killed by the hail of metal shrapnel. One man had the top of his head sliced off. He died instantly, folding at the knees and falling to the ground, his heels drumming a nerve spasming tattoo against the blacktop in a pool of thick dark blood.

Wayland ordered JJ to switch to coax and the machine gun that was slaved to the main barrel of the tank cut a murderous swathe through the trees and bushes by the side of the road. The power of the coaxial flensed the hedgerows of their foliage and killed every soldier concealed behind them. A Russian officer staggered to his feet in the aftermath of the fusillade, his face bloodied, his body riddled with a dozen wounds. He had lost his helmet but still his face was unrecognizable beneath a mask of blood. He waved his arm, urging his troops forward, but there were no men left alive to respond to his order. He turned, took a dazed, tottering last step, and then crumpled to the ground and did not move again. Another Russian soldier popped out from behind a tree with an RPG propped on his shoulder. Wayland identified the target and JJ swung the turret just in time to kill the man with a fusillade of machine gun fire before he could launch.

Sergeant McGrath's tank was not so fortunate. From behind one of the BMP-3s in a nearby field a second Russian soldier dashed from cover, dropped to his knee and fired an RPG. The missile struck the skirt of slat armor that encased the hull. The round exploded harmlessly against the outer barrier. McGrath's gunner took savage revenge, firing a HEAT round at the APC and destroying it.

The Irish infantry, too, were fighting valiantly. Heavily outnumbered, they were ruthless in their discipline, picking off enemy targets flushed out of cover by the charging Abrams'.

Quickly the momentum of the battle swung in favor of the allies. Wayland's aggressive charge had caught the Russians disorganized and off-balance. Virtually invulnerable to the small caliber guns of the APCs, the Abrams only threat was from hand held anti-tank missiles. Wayland kept JJ firing the coax until the two tanks crashed through the roadblock of shattered BMP-3s and the Americans found themselves amongst the enemy's ranks. The Russians began to fall back in alarm. Some men dropped their weapons and ran for distant farm houses. Others threw up their hands in surrender. Three of the BMP-3 commanders ordered their drivers to flee the battlefield, adding to the bedlam of noise, smoke and fire.

Wayland switched to the CROWS system (Common Remotely Operated Weapon Station) and fired on the enemy infantry with the Abrams' 50cal machine gun from within the turret. Sergeant McGrath ordered his gunner to open fire on the retreating APCs. The Irish infantry, sensing the enemy were abandoning their position, broke from cover and came forward in skirmish order. Two Irish soldiers went down in the attack, both of them killed by head shots. Another three were injured and fell in the long grass by the road.

Within minutes the battle was almost over. Almost, but not quite. The Irish infantry lost three more men before they reached the wreckage of the BMP-3s parked across the road.

They found dozens of dead and scores of badly wounded men who would not survive the night. The Abrams has wreaked untold carnage. The road had been splashed with blood and gore; the aftermath of the slaughter was gruesome. Bodies had been scorched, others torn apart. The air smelled of blood and burning flesh and diesel fumes. Thick columns of oily smoke climbed high into the afternoon sky. The injured sobbed pitifully and cried out for help.

Wayland stood in the open hatch of the turret and stared across the battlefield. Everywhere he looked there was a fresh horror – another chilling scene of ghastly devastation. Until now, so much of the combat for the village had been fought at a distance and between armored vehicles. But this… this was a close-up view of a hellish bloodbath.

He snatched off his CVC helmet. His face was dripping sweat and caked in a powder of dust and grime. He scraped the back of his hand across his brow and saw Sergeant McGrath emerge from the turret of his tank, fifty yards along the road. The two men looked at each other. There was no celebration, no euphoria. They had done their job, and done it with brutal efficiency – nothing more. The time for nightmares, remorse, and brooding reflection might come later, but for now there was still a village to be defended and thus more killing to be done.

Wayland gave the order to his driver, and the two Abrams turned back towards Stare Lubiejewo.

*

The scene Wayland encountered as the two Red Platoon Abrams' returned to Stare Lubiejewo was apocalyptic.

Many of the houses on the western side of the village had been reduced to rubble or were on fire. The smoke was so thick the sky had turned blood-red. Ash and dust hung in the air so the images of devastation were misted behind a hellish orange haze. But even the soft focus caused by the smoke could not conceal the evidence of savage fighting that had taken place in Wayland's absence. The school had been hit twice by Russian tank rounds. The northwest corner of the building had collapsed and the windows gaped like black open mouths, rimmed with soot, the glass shattered where fire had broken out. Most of the trees along the leafy streets had been flattened as though uprooted by a tornado. Power lines hung across the blacktop. All of the houses close to the intersection had been obliterated, the rubble of their remains strewn across the road so the area resembled a vast demolition site.

Between the chaos of ruined buildings were four destroyed T-90 tanks and an Abrams. Two of the Russian tanks had been split apart and still smoldered. The other two had burned out, blackened by soot. The air stank of oil and diesel… and death. The Abrams had been struck from behind. The rear of the vehicle was smashed in where the round had torn through the engine compartment and killed everyone on board. The round had pierced the tank's internal fuel bladder as it travelled through the hull ammunition compartment. The subsequent explosion had caused an uncontrollable fire that had ultimately burned the tank out. No one had survived.

Wayland surveyed the appalling scene with numb disbelief as he climbed down from his tank. Major Browne strode towards him.

"Eight of your infantry were killed clearing the road, I'm afraid. And five or six more were lightly wounded," Wayland reported somberly to the Irish officer.

Major Browne winced and looked genuinely distressed. He cupped his hands to his mouth. "Captain O'Malley!"

"Sir?" The infantry Captain appeared with his face caked in grey dust from within the ruins of a nearby building.

"Wounded? Killed?"

"Ten dead, sir, and another six wounded. The Americans lost another tank. They were lads from White Platoon."

"We're stretched pretty thin," Wayland understated bleakly. "Your infantry must be down to half strength by now, and we have, what? Eight tanks left from the original fourteen?" he blinked like a man waking from a nightmare. "I don't know how we can hold off another determined attack if the Russians decide to come at us again…"

Major Browne said nothing. The Russians must know how few men and tanks remained defending the village. Another assault seemed imminent.

An infantryman came up, looking anxious. "Captain Kohn is being attended to by the American medics behind the school, sir. The NCO asked me to fetch you. The Captain has regained consciousness and is calling for you both."

The tank Company's M113A3 APC Medic track was parked in the rear grounds of the school beneath a grove of trees. The ramp of the vehicle was down, revealing a tight interior crammed with essential medical equipment and four stretchers, two fitted to each interior side wall. Captain Kohn sat on the edge of the ramp, hunched over with his elbows on his knees and his bandaged head in his hands. His hair was stiff with dark dry blood. He turned, his expression volcanic with rage.

"Fuckin' Brody, the bastard," Captain Kohn launched into a vehement tirade. The bitter shame of defeat galled him. "It was his fault, damn it," Kohn seethed about Blue Platoon Leader, Scott Brody, who had died, along with his entire crew, in a ball of fire.

"Sir?" Wayland frowned.

"Brody! The cowardly bastard!" Kohn swore in a rising fit of outrage. "I ordered him to crest the skyline and fall upon the Russians. He was too slow! If he hadn't hesitated…"

Major Browne raised a discreet eyebrow at Wayland.

"Surely you saw it, Wayland!" Kohn went on, oblivious of the unsavoury glance the other two men exchanged. "You must have seen how Brody hesitated. It ruined my attack. If it wasn't for him…" he bit off the words and let out a long breath of exhaustion, fatigue and failure. When he spoke again, his voice was heavy but forceful. "There be a report, of course. I know the man is dead, but this kind of cowardice cannot be ignored. It will need to go on his record.

And when I notify Battalion, I expect your report will match exactly with mine, Lieutenant."

*

"Christ on his cross!" Major Browne hissed, aghast. "Your Captain Kohn's a feckin' gobshite eejit, so he is!"

Wayland arched his eyebrows. "Sir?"

"He's daft and reckless, and bloody arrogant, Lieutenant. He'll get us all killed."

Wayland made a pained face. "Yes."

The two men were standing in front of the school building by the Major's command Landrover. Browne sighed and looked to the sky as if the answer might be written in the smoke. He grimaced and then said delicately with a sideways glance, "We'll have to get rid of him…"

"Yes." Kohn's careless charge had been a disaster. Wayland suspected the Captain was trying to earn himself a medal to emerge from the shadows of his father and step-brothers' accomplishments. But his blind ambition had cost brave men their lives. He had to be stopped. "What do you suggest?"

"I'm the senior ranking officer," Browne said. "I can just relieve him of command."

"He won't go without a fight," Wayland warned. "His father and two step-brothers served, and all of them won medals. I think Kohn wants to emulate or exceed their successes. Relieving him of command would be the kind of black stain on his record that would ruin his career. It could get messy…"

"You have another idea?"

"Yes," Wayland steeled himself. "But let me talk to the medic alone first. Meet me back at the Medic track in ten minutes… and let me do all the talking."

*

When Wayland and Major Browne returned to the tank Company's M113A3 Medic track, they found Captain Kohn laying on a stretcher. He got to his feet. His eyes appeared dull and out of focus.

He turned his gaze on Wayland. "Have you prepared your report to Battalion, Wayland? I want to read it before you submit."

"I have not, sir," Wayland said.

"Then what do you want?" Kohn snapped.

"I want you to return to Warsaw with the injured, and any civilian evacuees. I want you to surrender command of the tank company."

Kohn stared, speechless, shock in his face. Wayland went on, and suddenly his tone turned brutal. "You attacked an unknown enemy across unknown terrain, and in doing so directly violated specific orders against the objections of both myself and Major Browne. As a consequence, men died needlessly and several tanks were destroyed. The aftermath of your reckless action resulted in a Russian counter-attack that caused even more death and destruction. Sir, you have a serious head wound. You need to return to Warsaw and leave the defence of the village in Major Browne's hands until we are relieved by reinforcements."

"I made the right tactical move," Kohn turned red-faced and belligerent. "Only Lieutenant Brody's cowardice – "

"No, sir," Wayland interrupted harshly. "Your action was unnecessarily rash. The fault for the attack was yours alone."

"I'll have you busted to a corporal for this insubordination, Wayland," Kohn blustered. "It's your word against mine, and how dare you – "

"No, sir," Wayland interrupted again, this time his voice rising to cut the Captain's tirade short. "Major Browne is prepared to file a report on the incident, and so am I. It's our word against yours."

"No, Wayland!"

"Yes, Captain. And if we file our reports, your career is over. You're finished. You'll never command again, never see action. Imagine the shame such an unseemly incident would bring on your family. How would your father feel, to know the son of a Vietnam medal winner was a rash fool responsible for the deaths of almost half his Company?"

In a single gasp of helpless impotence, the fight went from Kohn. His hands flapped and his face turned ghostly-white. He looked sideways at Major Browne and saw the unflinching steel of the Irishman's resolve. Kohn's shoulders slumped. He was trapped; faced with inevitable humiliation and a stain of shame he could never hope to expunge.

Wayland glanced about him to make sure the medics were not in earshot. "We have to hold this village, sir, and I don't think you're the man to command the Company. You'll kill us all to win your damned medals."

"Wayland?" Kohn began to plead.

"No," Wayland shook his head. "The best the Major and I am prepared to do is offer you the chance to keep your reputation intact. If you leave here right now with the rest of the injured and any civilians who want to evacuate, then there will be no report on what happened from me, or from Major Browne. I've spoken to the medic. He said your wound could be superficial, or it could be serious – head wounds are hard to diagnose. You've suffered a concussion. Your vision could go, you could collapse. You might have internal swelling or bleeding. No one will think less of you for being evacuated to Warsaw for urgent medical analysis."

"You're blackmailing me," Kohn made a last feeble attempt to fight back.

"Yes."

Kohn's expression became pitiful. He dabbed at the swathe of bandages wrapped around his forehead with his fingertips. "You'll say nothing about the attack?"

"You have our word. But you leave now."

Kohn couldn't bring himself to utter his concession. Instead he nodded his head in mute agreement.

The bedraggled caravan of civilian cars left from the hotel carpark thirty-five minutes later. Captain Kohn sat slumped in the back seat of the lead vehicle, escorted by a Company medic. In the cars that followed were injured Irish infantrymen and a handful of locals clutching their meagre possessions. Wayland did not watch the caravan leave and Captain Kohn did not look back as the vehicles drove away.

Not once.

*

"What time is it?" Wayland stretched his back and scraped his hand across his sweaty brow. He was filthy with dust and dirt.

"After three," Sergeant McGrath said. The men stood back from the worksite and cast their eyes across the intersection. The sky was an ominous red, filled with dust and ash. The afternoon sun shone like a fireball behind dense billows of smoke. The village appeared other-worldly – like a scene from a science fiction planet, backdropped by the eerie blood-red gloom.

It had been two hours of frantic effort since Captain Kohn and the wounded Irish infantry had been driven south to Warsaw with a straggle of civilian evacuees. Now, at last, Wayland felt preparations to defend the village were complete.

Two of the remaining eight Abrams had been dug in behind redoubts to defend the main intersection; one on either side of the road. With Kohn gone, the commander's tank had been parked hull down behind a crumbled stone wall and then camouflaged with thrown debris and building rubble to conceal and further protect it. Then more rocks and broken bricks had been brought to insulate the side armor. With just a three-man crew, the gunner would man the tank commander's station, leaving the loader still to load and the driver free to manoeuvre the vehicle. But the position of the tank had turned the Abrams into a virtual pill-box. It would only reverse out of danger if the Russians threatened to overrun the village.

The second tank was Wayland's, parked in the ruins of a house on the opposite side of the road. Here they had used two abandoned tractors to shield the tank's side armor and fortified the front of the hull behind the rubble of an old brick chimney. The two tanks would form the centre of the defensive line and hold the road north against enemy tanks. The rest of the remaining Abrams were similarly positioned hull-down in good defensive locations along the western streets. Wayland's plan could not call for a mobile defence; there simply weren't enough tanks to cover the village's most vulnerable points against a determined attack. Only Sergeant McGrath's Abrams would be kept in reserve, parked behind the ruins of the school building and able to dash to vulnerable points to shore up crumbling defences.

Wayland's greatest worry was ammunition. Sergeant McGrath gloomily reported that each tank had scarcely half their normal loadout left. The White Platoon tanks had a little more because they had not yet been heavily engaged in combat, but the grim total was far less than Wayland had hoped for. He made some mental calculations and grunted.

"I figure we've got enough for a twelve-minute battle. After that we're going to be in serious trouble."

He ordered McGrath to redistribute ammunition so the two vehicles at the crossroads and his reserve tank were well stocked with sabot rounds, and sent most of the available HEAT rounds to the tanks on the western edge of the village where he expected the Russians to attack again with their BMP-3s.

Major Brown and Captain O'Malley had been busy too, reorganizing the Irish infantry and the men of their precious Javelin anti-tank platoon. The eastern section of the village would be defended with just a handful of lightly wounded soldiers, while the remainder of the Irish company that were still fit to fight would take up positions around each tank. The Javelin teams were entrenched along the road running north to Lomza and on the western flank of the village, working from elevated positions amongst the ruined buildings.

"It's all we can do," Wayland shrugged as he cast one last troubled look across the intersection. "We just have to hold on until help arrives."

"Is help coming, sir?" Sergeant McGrath asked.

"Yes."

"When?"

Wayland shook his head. He had asked Captain Kohn the same question at the hotel. Now he was the one without answers. No one at Battalion or in Warsaw knew. "Soon. I hope."

The discussion was interrupted by the pounding feet of an Irish infantryman. He skidded to a halt on loose gravel, red faced and puffing. His eyes were red-rimmed with fatigue.

"Lieutenant Wayland?" the young soldier saluted quickly.

"Yes."

"Major Browne's regards, sir, and a message," he paused to draw a gasping breath. "Would you mind putting down the bloody shovel and meeting him at the school building. The bloody Russians look like they're up to something."

Wayland swore quietly and dashed for the school.

*

A few minutes after three o'clock a group of Russian officers appeared on the crest of the rise. Colonel Pugacheva had a chicken drumstick in his hand. He stared at the village in the distance, hunched beneath a smudge of black smoke. He finished eating, chewing loudly, and then lifted binoculars to his eyes. For long moments he scanned the outskirts of Stare Lubiejewo and saw nothing that alarmed him.

"Do you think the bastards have packed up and retreated to Warsaw?" he asked hopefully.

Alferov, the zampolit, stepped forward and stood at the Colonel's shoulder. "No."

Pugacheva made a sour face. "A pity," he said. "We've already paid too high a price for this worthless little hovel. It is a pimple, Alferov. A pimple on the ass of the world, and my men have died fighting for it. I still don't understand why."

"Because, Colonel," the zampolit's voice turned oily, "the village stands on a road to Warsaw and the Army behind us must be unobstructed."

Pugacheva grunted. He still had the binoculars pressed to his eyes. "They're very quiet. Like mice. I can see no movement."

"I assure you, Colonel, the enemy are still there. They've probably re-dug their defenses and are waiting for us."

"Then they are expecting us to attack again. What's the situation with our reserves?"

Alferov had the information memorized. "The rest of the battalion has begun to arrive. They're spilling off the road now and forming around the forest. I expect them to be ready for action in, perhaps an hour."

"What about my field artillery?"

"Four 2S1 Gvozdika's have arrived."

"Good," the Colonel allowed himself a brief smile. The Gvozdika's were self-propelled 122mm howitzers. Four was not enough, but it would do.

"And the rest of the Army?"

"The main Army is still many miles behind. They won't arrive until tonight, or maybe tomorrow morning."

Pugacheva growled. "Why so long?"

"Logistics, Colonel," the zampolit explained patiently, hiding his irritation. "The road is clogged for miles. They can't move any faster."

"And what about ground attack aircraft I was promised? Where the hell are our Su-25's?"

"There are no aircraft flying, Colonel. Command does not believe they have air superiority, and the recent rain... The Air Force is flying essential missions only. And the Su-25's right across the northern front have been hard hit by NATO. They can't be spared."

"Typical," the Colonel spat his contempt. "War is always won by men on the ground, Alferov. Remember that," the old

Colonel suddenly launched into a lecture. "No matter what technology, no matter how many planes or ships a nation has, it's always the fighting soldiers who matter most. The ground war determines the fate of nations."

"Indeed," the zampolit struggled to conceal his contempt for the old Colonel's arrogance. To Alferov, Pugacheva was a bombastic fool, caught up in grandiose memories of his past glories. Meanwhile the world had passed him by and now time was wasting. The Russians needed to secure the village and sweep aside the defenders.

"Are you planning another attack?" Alferov prompted.

"No," Pugacheva said and saw the disapproval on the zampolit's face. "We will wait until the rest of the Battalion is formed and ready for action. In the meantime," he smiled foxily, "I think we should have a little talk with our enemy and let them know the hell we are about to unleash. Maybe they will see reason and surrender. It would save us all a lot of trouble. See to it, Alferov. I want you to lead the delegation. You know what to say."

Chapter 7:

"So, what do you make of that?" Major Browne pointed towards the northern horizon and then handed Wayland a pair of binoculars. The men were standing on the roof of the school building, well away from the bomb-damaged northwest corner that looked like it could collapse at any moment.

Wayland took the binoculars and focused them on the distant skyline. First, he picked out a clumped fringe of trees, and then he drew the lenses along the crest in a slow sweep until he suddenly saw a Russian P-230T all-terrain command-staff vehicle appear, trailing a tail of dust. The vehicle was a high, box-shaped four-wheel drive, painted in camouflage colors. From out of the passenger-side window had been thrust a long pole, and attached was a white bedsheet, flapping in the breeze. Wayland gaped. A moment later a second similar vehicle appeared on the rise, following the first in convoy.

Wayland put down the binoculars and glanced at the Irish Major, his surprise showing. "Well, assuming they're not surrendering to us," Wayland said wryly, "I suppose they want to talk."

"Yes," Major Browne frowned. "Bloody suspicious if you ask me. The bastards are up to something. But perhaps we can turn this into an opportunity?"

"Major?"

"I've just been on the radio to Warsaw. Reinforcements are on their way, but they're not going to arrive until tomorrow morning."

Wayland looked appalled. "Do they know how desperate our situation is?"

"Yes. I've told them. But tomorrow is the earliest. The roads between here and Warsaw are a refugee-choked nightmare… and the reinforcements coming to our aid aren't actually in Warsaw yet."

"What? Who is coming to relieve us?"

"The bloody French, so they are!" Major Browne sounded aghast. "Command is sending a column of twenty-two Leclerc tanks and thirty-six VBCI Armored Infantry Fighting

Vehicles. They're the advance element of the French Army's 2nd Armored Brigade. They're due to arrive on the outskirts of Warsaw sometime this evening, and they'll be re-routed around the city and pushed forward to us."

Wayland took a moment to process the information. The French Leclerc was a fine tank – more than a match for the Russian T-90 – and the French Army was modern, well-trained and well-equipped. But none of that would matter if the village could not be defended until they arrived.

"So, we've got to buy time," Wayland understood grimly. "We've got to do everything we can to delay the Russians from attacking for as long as possible."

"Quite."

"Fine," Wayland nodded, his decision made. "I'll go and talk to the bastards and see what they have to say."

"Actually, I was going to go."

"You can't, sir," Wayland appealed to the Irishman's common sense. "If it's a trap, you'll be killed and the village will fall. I'll go in your place. Can I borrow your Landrover?"

"Certainly," Browne nodded. "I'll send a driver with you to make sure you don't damage Her Majesty's military equipment. Everyone knows you Yanks are loons behind a steering wheel. Anything else you need?"

"Yeah," Wayland rubbed his chin drolly and cast one final baleful glance at the approaching convoy of Russian vehicles. "Can you get a couple of snipers to cover me? I don't want to be killed either…"

*

The two Russian vehicles stopped in the middle of a plowed field a kilometer from the village. Wayland sat in the passenger seat of the Landrover as the young driver flung the vehicle across the open ground. The ride was appalling; the vehicle jounced and bucked and squeaked over every pothole and depression so that Wayland wondered if the vehicle had been built without suspension.

The driver braked to a halt fifty yards from the Russian vehicles.

"Keep the engine running," Wayland said and climbed out. He stepped warily towards the enemy.

There were four men waiting for him. Two young drivers stood miserably in the background and two officers stepped forward. The first man wore the uniform of a Russian infantry Captain. He had a florid, fleshy face and a wide petulant slash for a mouth. He had his hand resting casually on the grip of his sidearm. He eyed Wayland with wary suspicion.

The second man wore a non-descript knee-length military overcoat, black polished boots and black leather gloves. He was thin featured and pallid. His clammy skin showed the pock-marks of childhood acne scars. His eyes were dark and unblinking; a mocking, reptilian countenance of veiled hostility. His flat snakelike eyes moved slowly over Wayland's face and uniform. He nodded his head and gave a thin arrogant smile that looked more like a sneer.

"My name is Alferov," he said. "Major Alferov." His tone was high-pitched and reedy, his English thick.

"Wayland," the tank platoon leader said. "Lieutenant Wayland."

The Russian seemed mildly perplexed, though he took great pains to conceal his expression. "Only a Lieutenant? Surely you do not command the defense of the village?"

"No," Wayland guessed the Russian to be in his late thirties or early forties. "The commanding officer is Major Browne of the Irish Guards."

The Russian made a pantomime of pretending to looking past Wayland's shoulder towards the distant village. "Where is he?"

"Busy," Wayland put some bite into his voice. "We captured a lot of your infantry during your failed attempts to seize the settlement, and the Major is interrogating them all. He sends his regards."

The Russian blinked; a split-second falter of the fixed façade on his face that revealed Wayland's barb had struck home. The man took a moment to compose himself but when he smiled again the expression was strained. "You speak on the Major's authority?"

"Yes. Do you speak with the authority of your Lieutenant Colonel Pugacheva?" Wayland followed up with a short jab.

The remnants of the smile on the Russian's face froze and then slid away. His eyes became hooded and dangerous. His mood became brusque. He pulled off his gloves and flexed his fingers, then reached into an inside pocket of his long coat.

"My Colonel wants to inform you that your men have fought gallantly and that you have done your nations proud. He wishes for there to be no more unnecessary bloodshed. We both know you are vastly outnumbered and that your situation is hopeless. This," he held out an envelope, "contains a written guarantee from my Colonel that every allied soldier currently defending the village of Stare Lubiejewo will be afforded all the protections of the Geneva Convention should they lay down their weapons and surrender to our Army immediately."

Wayland accepted the envelope and tucked it into a pocket. "I shall take your offer to Major Browne for his consideration," Wayland said formally. "But I doubt he will accept. Instead of saying more, Wayland pointedly looked around the vast expanse of farm fields that were littered with the smoldering wrecks of destroyed Russian personnel carriers. "So far we've had no trouble fighting off your attacks."

"So far, you have been lucky," Alferov sneered.

"Maybe."

"But your luck will soon run out, American. The rest of our Battalion is arriving as we speak and before nightfall the entire Russian Army will be massed beyond that rise. To this point we have merely probed your defenses. A single concerted attack will leave every man defending that village slaughtered."

"Maybe," Wayland kept his expression neutral and taunting. "But if you had the troops you needed to take the village, you would have attacked by now – and you wouldn't be here trying to negotiate a surrender with me. And you're not the only one expecting reinforcements. Within an hour a whole column of French tanks and APCs will be arriving to reinforce the village."

Now it was the Russian's turn to narrow his eyes in sly mockery. "I don't believe you, Lieutenant."

Wayland shrugged his shoulders. "I don't care if you believe me. I don't believe you either."

Alferov sniffed. The air was still thick with smoke. It irritated his eyes. "I expect your answer regarding our terms of surrender within thirty minutes."

Wayland shook his head. "No. I'll give you our answer in two hours. We will need that long to consider your offer."

Alferov was too cunning to fall for a blatant stalling tactic. "If your answer is not received within thirty minutes, Lieutenant, we will assume you have rejected our terms and there will be no more subsequent offers. You will be directly responsible for the death of every man defending that village."

*

"We've got less than half an hour to surrender," Wayland reported back to Major Browne. The Irish officer had watched the meeting through high-powered binoculars from the rooftop of the school building. "Otherwise the Russians have threatened to slaughter every man defending the village. Here," he handed over the envelope containing the Russian offer. Browne put the document in his pocket without looking at it.

"What else did they say?"

"That they have reinforcements arriving, and that the rest of the Russian spearhead is on its way down the road from Lomza. They claim the entire Army will be ready to attack before nightfall."

Browne went to the edge of the rooftop and swept his eyes along the skyline, standing there in the soldier's stance, balanced on the balls of his feet with his hands clasped behind his back. The view was uninspiring. The fires burning throughout the village had been brought under control, but still the sky was filled with black smoke. Along the rubble-strewn streets soldiers moved quietly from dug-out to dug-out, distributing ammunition and passing around canteens of water. Browne watched without really seeing any of it. He squared his shoulders and turned back to Wayland.

"Play Devil's Advocate for a moment, Lieutenant. Tell me why we should surrender."

Wayland thought carefully before finally speaking. "We're down to half strength. You've lost forty or fifty good men, and my tank company has lost six out of fourteen Abrams. The troops are exhausted, and they're scared. They've fought bitterly to hold the Russians off and no more could be expected of them. We've got wounded that need medical attention and we're running low on supplies and ammunition. If the Russians come again, and if they break through, they'll be merciless. The men know the enemy just offered terms for our surrender. They'll be thinking about it and wondering to themselves whether this god-forsaken little village is worth dying for. That kind of thinking gnaws away at a man's confidence. They know we're outnumbered and that there is no hope of reinforcements until at least tomorrow morning. You're asking them to endure another eighteen hours of hell which very few of them can expect to survive. And in the end? What will it all have been for?"

Browne nodded. In truth, he had been plagued by the same thoughts, struggling to find a balance between the logical hopelessness of their situation and the pride of a fighting man who never admitted defeat. But if they surrendered, the war would be over for them. They would likely end up in a baren Russian prisoner-of-war camp somewhere deep inside Russia. They might never be released. If the Russians won the war, they might be executed. Was he acting any better than Captain Kohn if he bloody-mindedly continued to fight on, careless of the casualties that would be inflicted?

The Irish Major stared down at the ground for a long moment. When he lifted his face again, his features had changed. He appeared older, greyer.

"I have a wife and five children," he confessed in a quiet voice. "They're back home in Sallynoggin. It's a little village southeast of Dublin. Every weekend we'd take a family drive to Dun Laoghaire by the seaside and eat ice cream in the park. Most of the men in this Company have families…"

Wayland narrowed his eyes. "What are you worried about, Major? Dying in battle, or being taken prisoner and never seeing your family again?"

Major Browne blinked. Wayland's question had been deliberately harsh and provocative.

"I'm worried about being taken prisoner and never seeing my family again. And I worry about the selfishness of choosing to fight on for that reason, because it's going to cost a lot of men their lives," he agonized.

"You think you're fighting on for the wrong reason?"

"Yes. I think I'm fighting on for personal reasons… Maybe I'm no better than Captain Kohn."

Wayland smiled thinly but there was no humor in his eyes. "And you expect me to be sympathetic?"

Major Browne said nothing.

Wayland swept his gaze across the intersection. The wind had changed, blowing the smoke from the smoldering village ruins away to the south. "We're fighting here because we're good at it, and we're fighting because the Russians think they should rule Europe. You knew the hazards of this work long before this war started. You might be a family man also, but right now you're a soldier. A damned good one; the best I've ever worked with. And if you do your job properly, more of the men you command will live to be reunited with their families one day. But if you let them down… if your resolve to resist the Russians weakens because you're undecided – you'll get us all slaughtered. There no compromise in war. It's either kill or be killed."

Browne blinked. He had expected Wayland to be sympathetic to his quiet moment of vulnerability. Now he felt ashamed for his weakness. "You're right," he said and straightened his shoulders.

"As a soldier, you're fighting on because you have orders to defend this village. If you didn't have a family, would you even consider surrendering?"

"No."

"Then you have your answer, and it's the same for every other man fighting here. Right now, we're all just soldiers, and our duty is to carry out our orders."

Major Browne nodded acceptance of Wayland's sage insight and his face flushed with color. Wayland sensed the Irishman's embarrassment. The American brushed the moment aside and raised his voice, changing the subject. "Now," he drew a breath. "What else can we do to give those Russian bastards a bloody nose the next time they attack us?"

*

Colonel Pugacheva listened to Alferov's report and felt a moment of idle regret. It would have been simpler if the enemy had straightaway accepted his terms of surrender.

"You say they're commanded by an Irishman?"

"Yes. A Major Browne of the Irish Guards," the zampolit answered.

"But the man you spoke to was an American tanker?"

"Yes. A Lieutenant."

Pugacheva frowned. He took a final sip of his coffee and then tossed the dregs into the grass. Behind him the Battalion was amassing, spilling off the road from Lomza and forming up across the wide flat depression beyond sight of the enemy. With the arrival of his remaining tank and APC companies, the Colonel felt confident that one more determined charge would overwhelm the enemy. After a few brief moments of resistance, the battle would be over, and the village his.

"You gave them thirty minutes to respond to our offer?"

"Yes, Colonel," Alferov checked his watch. "Time is almost up."

The Colonel walked through long grass to the crest of the rise and pulled binoculars to his eyes. He could see no sign of activity in the village.

"It doesn't look like they're going to accept…"

"Nor would I have expected it, Colonel," the zampolit admitted. "The American was an arrogant bastard. Not the kind to surrender or be intimidated easily."

Pugacheva grunted. "Then there's no point wasting any more time on politeness. We'll attack them now and be done with the damned business before sunset. Give the orders, Alferov. Get the tanks and troop carriers moving immediately."

*

Major Browne watched the distant billowing clouds of dust from the rooftop of the school building and recognized the ominous threat they promised. Far to the north the dust rose high in the still air like smoke from a bush fire burning across a wide front. The Major licked dry cracked lips and fidgeted with his radio.

MREs had been distributed through the ranks but most of the men were too fraught with tension to eat. Then the Russian artillery opened fire, raining howitzer rounds down on the defenders from over the horizon. One round landed on the roof of a barn at the eastern end of the village and blew the building to pieces.

A sniper lying prone on the rooftop beside the Major began to cough incessantly. Birds in a nearby tree took to sudden panicked flight.

Down in the trenches, and in the ruined buildings, soldiers checked their weapons and exchanged morbid jokes as their anxiety bubbled to the surface.

Finally the ground-trembling rumble of approaching Russian armor could be heard – the ominous clamor punctuated by artillery fire that had begun like spattered raindrops and then quickly turned into a deluge until the sky seemed filled with their shrieking whine. The ground shuddered with every fresh explosion.

From inside his tank by the intersection, Wayland could see very little. But his instincts told him an attack was imminent. The Russians, he knew, would attack en masse, for it was the Russian way of war; the method that had brought victory to the Red Army during the campaigns of the Second World War. They would hurl themselves at the village like an avalanche of steel and guns, overwhelming the defenders with targets and riding over the dead on their irresistible way to triumph. Casualties would be heavy, but that was a small consideration to the Russians. Victory was all that mattered.

"Swanny, load sabot…"

"Up!" Specialist Wayne Swan rammed a round into the breach in record time, infected by the rising tension.

Wayland spoke across the Platoon net, calling Captain Kohn's tank on the opposite side of the road. The Abrams was now being commanded by the gunner.

"Black Six, Red One. Remember the plan. You don't fire until I do, and then you give it everything you've got."

"Red One, Black Six, confirm," the gunner's voice squeaked in the headphones of Wayland's CVC helmet.

Inside Wayland's Abrams the crew were tense and sweating. The tank's engine was running, drowning out ambient sound from beyond the steel hull, but still the tension was a palpable thing that thickened the air as the seconds drew out.

Another Russian howitzer round crashed down on the village, overshooting the intersection by a hundred yards. It gouged a smoldering crater out of the blacktop and flung debris against the steel of Wayland's tank like a handful of thrown gravel against a window.

The air above the western farm fields seemed to shimmer. Then it filled with blooms of dirty brown smoke. They blossomed, then merged on the light breeze until they hung above the ground like a low cloud.

"They're coming!" Major Browne spoke across his company net to raise the alert, macabrely relieved the anxiety of waiting was over. "All troops standby to open fire. Engage enemy targets at will!"

Across the skyline to the west of the village the ground suddenly erupted with a terrifying phalanx of BMP-3 armored fighting vehicles. They came like a wall of steel, seeming to rise up from out of the ground, the smoke haze mixing with the black belching exhaust of their growling engines. They advanced at high speed, holding their formation until they encountered the first hedgerows. There the faster vehicles pulled ahead of those forced to negotiate the obstacle, and the implacable irresistible wall broke apart and became the wild mayhem of a blood-shivering madman's charge.

From a thousand yards north of the village where the road to Lomza kinked in a sharp corner, T-90 tanks suddenly appeared. The sleek steel monsters were travelling at high speed, barreling along the road in a column, hemmed in on either side by the tall leafy trees that splashed them in flickers of sunlight and shadow as they raced nearer.

Wayland took a deep breath and held it. He could feel the small insects of his fear crawl along the taught sinews of his nerves. He waited until the lead tanks reached the destroyed ruins of the T-90 in the middle of the road. The first Russian tank veered left to swerve around the obstacle.

"Designate tank!"

"Up!" Swanny cried. There was already a sabot round in the breach.

"Identified!" J.J engaged the target.

"Fire and adjust!"

"On the way!"

The round hit the T-90 as it angled off the road, striking the enemy tank flush on the hull. The tank disappeared behind a blinding flash of flame and then grey black smoke enveloped it, rising high into the afternoon sky. Behind the veil of oily haze, the tank shuddered, slammed sideways by the force of the impact. Metal debris was flung into the air and then the tank seemed to sink on its suspension. Smoke spewed from the turret and stained the sky.

"Target!"

A few seconds later Kohn's Abrams fired, striking a second T-90 that had swerved right. The shot tore the turret clean off the Russian vehicle. A fiery dragon's breath of flame engulfed the tank. The explosion rumbled through the ground like an earthquake. The turret was blown sky-high, cartwheeling fifty feet into the air, trailing an arc of fire and sparks and burning debris. Dust and smoke billowed, and the brutal sound of the explosion seemed to slam like a fist against the air.

With two well-aimed close-range shots the road from Lomza was blocked, forcing the following vehicles in the column to dexterously negotiate the shoulder of the road between the palisade of trees. The Russians spilled into fields east of the village littered with the ruins of BMP-3s. Wayland felt a split-second of relief; his first objective had been achieved. Without access to the road, the enemy could not surge directly into the village.

Specialist Wayne Swan concentrated on reloading a fresh round of sabot into the breach; working with fast, practiced hands. He knocked the ammunition door switch with his knee, forcing it to slide open, then reached for a sabot round. Twisting at the waist, with the round cradled in both arms, he laid the munition on the stub-base of the open breach, lined it up, and drove it home with the knuckles of his bunched fist. The breach closed automatically. Swanny instinctively hunkered into a corner to avoid the wicked recoil, checked the 'safe-on' light on a panel by his left ear, and called out in a loud, urgent voice, "Up!"

The process took under seven seconds.

There were no fresh targets. The Russians had scattered amongst the farmhouse buildings at the northern fringes of the village. Wayland peered hard at his CITV screen for long tense seconds and then finally saw a T-90 flash across his front.

The tank slewed back and forth across the road like it was out of control, mud and dirt flung high into the air from its grinding steel tracks. The enemy tank's turret traversed until it pointed directly to where Wayland's Abrams crouched.

"Designate tank!"

"Identified!" Gunner J.J. Brown engaged the target and centered the sight reticle.

"Fire and adjust!" Wayland gave the command.

J.J. thumped the trigger. "On the way!"

The Abrams lurched back on its suspension and a shudder ran through the tank as the round left the barrel at supersonic speed behind a leaping jet of muzzle blast.

The sabot round was essentially a modern-day arrow. Without explosive power, the ammunition relied on piercing enemy tank armor with sheer momentum. The heart of the round was the penetrator; a narrow rod of depleted uranium with a pointed nose and stabilizing fins. The rear of the penetrator rod was attached to a propellant case, and the pointed front attached to the sabot structure to keep the penetrator centered within the barrel.

Once fired, the propellant casing remained in the chamber. The flimsy sabot structure fell away from the penetrator as soon as the round exploded from the barrel leaving the penetrator to plunge like a stake through the heart of the targeted vehicle, creating a lethal hail of metal fragments.

The sabot round struck the T-90 broadside. A huge skirt of grey smoke exploded outwards from around the hull, spreading fifty feet in every direction and enveloping the vehicle for long seconds. The tank stopped dead on its tracks, and when the smoke began to clear Wayland saw that several of the T-90's road wheels had been destroyed. A few moments later a tongue of orange flame leaped from one of the sprung turret hatches and danced across the smoldering hull. No one scrambled from the stricken vehicle. The flames grew fiercer and then dark black smoke boiled up from the interior.

"Target!" J.J declared.

The road north appeared suddenly empty. Nothing moved. Frustrated, Wayland turned his attention to the fields west of the village where the swarm of charging Russian BMP-3s were carrying their cargoes of troops towards imminent victory.

*

When the Russian armored personnel carriers were within five hundred yards of the village's western outskirts, the howitzers supporting the advance suddenly stopped firing.

To the beleaguered Irish infantry hunkered down in the ruins of the buildings and in deeply-dug trenches, it seemed suddenly oddly quiet. But it was not a real silence; the Abrams tanks defending the street still fired, and so did the Javelin teams. Eight of the BMP-3s that had begun the attack were already smoldering ruins, their blackened carcasses scattered across the battlefield.

Captain O'Malley, who commanded the infantry facing the attack, ran, doubled-over, from building to building pointing out targets and encouraging his men to calmness.

"Wait until the APCs stop and the doors open, to be sure. That's when you open fire on the bastards, lads. Don't waste ammunition. Wait until you see running men to shoot at," he kept his voice matter-of-fact.

The three closest BMP-3s slewed to a halt in the long muddy grass beyond the first line of hedgerows and nine armed men exploded from out of each carrier's rear steel doors. They scattered quickly, drifting in and out of sight through a dirty brown wall of smoke.

Parked behind a fence in the middle of the street, the American tank Company's M1064A3 mortar carrier suddenly opened fire, lobbing 120mm mortar shells into the fields. The ground erupted in fountains of muddy dirt and the first enemy soldiers began to fall as the four-man crew quickly settling into a killing rhythm.

"Fire!" Captain O'Malley shouted.

A Russian carrying a machine gun was hit in the forehead. The man jerked back as if plucked by invisible strings. The heavy weapon he carried fell to the ground as the soldier toppled over. For a brief moment the air around his head was tinged with a pink mist.

An Irish Corporal, hit by wild panicked fire from a Russian rifle, stared at the bleeding hole in his shoulder like it was a nuisance and then frowned with sudden puzzlement as his legs collapsed beneath him. He fell to the bottom of the muddy trench he had been fighting from and died choking on his own blood.

"Fire!"

One of the BMP-3s fired its main gun at a house in the middle of the street and O'Malley spun to see the building collapse. There had been a Javelin team operating from the ruins. Now the site was shrouded in black smoke.

"Fire!"

A two-man Javelin team operating from the second story bedroom of a house identified one of the stationery enemy personnel carriers five hundred yards away and the gunner set the cursor on the CLU (Command Launch Unit). He selected the 'direct-path' attack mode. The hum of the system's battery began to warble in his ear. Two track gate icons appeared in the monitor's site view. The gunner adjusted the width and the height of the gates until the target was framed and activated the missile lock. The operator took a last deep, settling breath – and squeezed the trigger.

The Javelin leaped against his shoulder and an exhaust of flames and smoke shrouded the team in billowing dust. The missile flew like an arrow and struck the BMP-3 broadside. The impact of the hit rocked the vehicle sideways and blew it apart. A searing flash of fire turned into brown mushroom of smoke. The men inside the vehicle were killed instantly, but three more Russian troop carriers safely unloaded their cargo of soldiers under the cover of machine gun fire. Soon the fields beyond the village were swarming with the menace of dark-shaped infantry.

The Irish troops, knowing their very survival depended on the speed and efficiency of their work, opened fire on the Russian soldiers before they could scramble into the soft cover of the hedgerows. Two of the Abrams tanks defending the western edge of the village ceased firing HEAT rounds and opened up with their coax machine guns.

Wayland watched the battle developing from the turret of his Abrams and was stunned at the appalling punishment the Russians were able to absorb, yet still press home their attack. Almost half the APCs that began the charge across the farm fields had been destroyed. The remainder had reached the hedgerows and disgorged their troops. Now the vehicles were supporting the infantry's advance with their turret-mounted 100mm guns while the troops took up the final phase of the assault, dashing forward under heavy fire to edge remorselessly closer to the nearest buildings.

Wayland identified the closest BMP-3 through his CITV and barked the order. "Designate PC. Load HEAT!"

"Up!" Swanny shouted. In the few seconds it took to load the round, the enemy APC had begun to disgorge its cargo of soldiers. They scrambled out the back of the stationery vehicle as the BMP-3 commander fired smoke grenades to conceal its position. The infantry section fanned out into the long grass and then a Sergeant rose bravely to his feet and urged his men forward.

"Identified!" J.J snapped. The Abrams' fire control system made the complex calculations.

"Fire and adjust!"

"On the way!"

The round slammed into the APC, tearing through the left-side roadwheels, shattering the steel track, and then punching through the hull armor beyond. For a split second nothing seemed to happen – and then the vehicle erupted in a fierce wall of towering fire. Two of the nearby infantrymen were shredded by flying debris and killed instantly. A third Russian had his right arm severed. He fell writhing to the ground, gushing blood, clutching with his free hand at the ragged stump where his other arm had been. The man made a ghastly sound of agony and then fell into the grass screaming in shock and pain.

"Target!" J.J declared.

Wayland had already swung his attention to the next APC by the hedgerow and called the target. Ten seconds later the BMP-3 was a burning wreck of twisted metal.

"Fire!" Captain O'Malley shouted, and the Irish infantry rallied for one final firefight. The closest Russians were laying prone in the long grass, less than two hundred yards from the outskirt buildings. They were shooting and moving, creeping inexorably closer beneath a heavy umbrella of suppressing fire.

"Fire!" The Irish infantry edged from cover to face down the threat. A Russian Corporal was shot twice in the leg and spun round before collapsing. The man beside him clutched at his arm and grimaced in pain, then fired wildly into the smoke-filled sky as he tumbled backwards.

From the rooftop of the school building the two snipers armed with L115A3 long range rifles went about their deadly trade with brutal efficiency, picking off Russian officers that revealed themselves behind the hedgerow. But it was not enough. The weight of the enemy's advance seemed relentless.

Wayland had waited until the last moment, believing the Irish infantry would be able to hold the Russians back, and now he worried that he had waited too long. He had hoped the APCs could have been stopped before the infantry were delivered to the battle. He keyed the Platoon net. "Red Four! Western side of the village, now! Infantry advancing towards the outskirt buildings. Bring the rage!"

Parked behind the school building, his Abrams tank engine running, Sergeant McGrath had been monitoring the chaos of combat through the comms in his CVC helmet. He gave the order to his driver and set his gunner to the coax machine gun.

The Abrams surged across the rear carpark, crashed through a wooden fence, and then jounced over the road. The tank raced forward, reached the intersection and swerved left into the fields like a wolf amongst a flock of scattering sheep.

The APCs beyond the hedgerow saw the Abrams and their turrets turned. The first gun fired but the round whanged off the tank's armor harmlessly. McGrath ignored the fire and concentrated on the enemy infantry spread out in the tall grass before him.

"Gunner, coax troops!"

The vehicle's gunner had already switched controls to activate the machine gun. The weapon's vacuum whined to life.

"Identified!" the range was just a few hundred meters.

"Fire and adjust!"

"On the way!"

The machine gun aboard the Abrams erupted into chattering short bursts. The enemy infantry saw the steel beast bearing down on them. Some of the Russians sprang to their feet and charged forward but they were cut down by the waiting Irish. Others broke cover and fell back in terror and disarray. The coax scythed them down like harvested wheat.

Another swarm of Russian infantry were still in the hedgerows, gathering themselves like a wave about to break across a beach. As the Sergeant commanding the attack sprang to his feet and waved his arm high above his head, McGrath called the new target.

"Gunner, coax troops!"

The turret swung towards the hedgerow. The instant the operator saw the looming threat he crushed the range finder button with his thumb.

"Identified!" Two hundred and fifty meters.

"Fire and adjust!"

"On the way!"

Another savage staccato of tracer bullets spewed from the muzzle of the coax, tearing the imminent attack apart. The Sergeant was the first to die, almost cut in half by the awesome firepower of the tank's machine gun. The flurry of savagery shredded the hedges and killed half the men poised to attack. One soldier was shot in the chest and thumped back, astonishment in his eyes and his upper body awash with bright blood. Another had his foot severed and fell into the grass sobbing, white-faced and twitching.

A second BMP-3 fired its main gun at the Abrams, striking the vehicle on the side of the turret from point blank range. The tank disappeared behind a bloom of black smoke but emerged, its engine snarling, its thick armor scorched and scarred but intact. The coaxial machine gun barked again and again, flickering tongues of bright flame like a dragon on the rampage.

Finally the Russian attack lost momentum and began to falter. Two of the BMP-3s reversed back into the open fields, still firing as they began the retreat. Wayland's tank destroyed one of the fleeing vehicles. The remaining Russian infantry broke ranks and began to inch backwards.

"You've got them on the run!" Captain O'Malley sensed victory had been snatched from the jaws of imminent defeat and his voice was a cheer of exultant relief. "Now kill the bastards! Kill them!" Men worked their weapons and reloaded with the mechanical efficiency born of their training and desperation. Three more Russian soldiers fell in the long grass and one died at the hedgerow as he ran for his life. McGrath's Abrams turned its fury on a reversing BMP-3 and blew it apart with a shot from close range that obliterated the vehicle behind a crimson red fireball.

Spot fires burned in the dry grass, ignited by flaming debris. Shredded smoke skeins drifted across the battlefield, twitched apart by a relentless fusillade of Irish light arms fire. A dozen APCs burned black oily smoke. And through it all men screamed, and bled and died in despair. One wounded Russian crawled into a shallow ditch and stared, bewildered, down at the stumps of his missing legs before shooting himself to escape the tormenting agony. Another teetered like a drunk, dazed and disoriented. He had been shot twice in the stomach. With one hand he clutched at his spilling guts and with the other he carried his rifle like a crutch, gulping for air like a landed fish.

"Leave him!" O'Malley barked. "He's a deadun'. Finish the rest of the bastards off!" His mouth was dry, gritted with dust and swirling ash, his face a mask of sweat and grime so that his teeth showed pearl-white. The whole battlefield became just a few short yards of swirling smoke and fire and deafening noise that hammered each man senseless until they fought in a daze, driven by habit and heart-stopping terror.

The Russian infantry suddenly broke and ran, and still the Irish infantry and the coax machine guns of the Abrams tanks hunted them mercilessly. A soldier slipped on spilt brains and dislocated his shoulder when he fell. His comrades ran past him, ignoring his agonized pleas for help.

Wayland, no more enemy visible from the monitor of his CITV, flung himself back in his command seat, dripping sweat and exhausted. But across the Company net the chaos continued unabated. Wayland tried to decipher the thick Irish accents. He could make out only a few words, but they chilled him with icy dread. The Russian T-90s that had spilled off the road from Lomza were now breaking into the eastern outskirts of the village…

The battle to save Stare Lubiejewo was still not over.

*

The sky had turned black with smoke. Major Browne peered through the swirling haze and tried to discern the state of the battle in the fields west of the village. The sound of gunfire and the heavy retort of the Abrams' guns seemed unrelenting. The air stank of cordite and oil. Dust and ash and burned leaves hung suspended in the smog. The wind picked up so that he had to shield his eyes with the back of his hand.

He watched Sergeant McGrath's tank burst into the farm fields and almost single-handedly thwart the Russian infantry's advance. Then he saw two more BMP-3s swallowed by fireballs and smoke. The sounds of machine gun fire became sporadic. He saw the dark flitting shapes of Russian infantry running in retreat and breathed a shallow sigh of relief…

"Sir?" one of the snipers turned his head and looked north with a puzzled frown.

"What is it?"

"East of that farmhouse," the man pointed. "Near the shoulder of the road. I thought I saw something."

Major Browne peered into the smoke but saw nothing. He turned back to the west in time to see another Russian BMP-3 explode. Suddenly the Irish sniper's voice was thick with shock.

"Jaysus! Enemy tanks!"

Major Browne turned in alarm. "Christ on his cross!" A thousand yards away Russian T-90s were trundling towards outlying farm buildings, past the burned out ruins of destroyed BMP-3s. There were only two Abrams from White Platoon defending the village east of the road. Major Browne counted at least eight T-90s. The attack came from across the same fields where earlier Russian infantry and tanks had broken into the network of narrow streets and destroyed Sergeant Rye's Abrams before being turned back by stoic defense. Now the tanks were coming again.

The two Abrams were parked on the street directly in front of the school building. Browne issued an urgent warning across the company net but the American tanks were already on the move, alerted to the threat by their onboard BMS systems. One Abrams surged forward, jouncing off the street onto uneven ground, barging towards the danger. Houses and farm buildings stood in the way. The Abrams followed a narrow dirt driveway between two barns and came out onto a concrete pad that provided parking spaces for nearby apartment buildings. Through a wall of trees, the vehicle's commander could see the ghostly outline of moving Russian tanks ploughing their way across a farm field. The tanks were rushing towards a row of hedges. The Abrams gunner locked onto a target and the American tank fired, killing the T-90. The Russian vehicle stopped abruptly and from its turret blew a funnel of black smoke. The Abrams commander locked onto a second enemy tank, but before he could fire, the Abrams was shaken by a direct hit that slammed into the turret. The vehicle's sophisticated armor saved the tank from destruction. The gunner located the enemy tank that had fired and changed targets. The T-90 was nestled in a grove of trees on the edge of an old football field. The Abrams fired but the shot deflected off the Russian vehicle's armor. The ricochet felled two nearby trees and brought a rain of dislodged leaves down on the enemy tank. The Russian fired back, scoring another hit on the Abrams, this time a strike on the front quarter of the hull. The sabot round pierced the Abrams armor and killed everyone inside. Major Browne heard the exchange of gunfire and saw the towering column of smoke begin to boil into the sky. He knew instantly that the Abrams had been killed.

"Red Four! Red Four! Eastern side of the village. T-90s at the outskirts. One Abrams destroyed!"

Sergeant McGrath heard the urgent call in his CVC helmet and barked at his driver. The tank turned in the muddy blood-stained fields and dashed towards the main road.

"Hell!" Wayland heard the call too. "Black Six, hold your position!" Wayland needed at least one tank to defend the intersection in case there were more Russian T-90s waiting to advance down the road. He ordered his driver to reverse from behind the redoubt and his tank dashed east.

Wayland and Sergeant McGrath saved the village. Together they surged across the main road and caught the Russian tanks in the flank from close range. The enemy were advancing cautiously, two vehicles crossing a football field and approaching the first row of houses while the rest of the formation overwatched their advance from behind hedgerows. When Wayland and McGrath's tanks appeared from the direction of the main road, the Russians were caught utterly by surprise.

The two American tanks had just seconds to drive home their advantage. They opened fire on the nearest enemy vehicles and caught them broadside. The low bushy hedgerow provided no cover. The first T-90 had its turret ripped clean off the hull by the savage impact of Wayland's first sabot round. The top blew off the enemy tank and cartwheeled into the air trailing a long tail of flames and sparks. McGrath's first shot slammed into the next T-90 and the round pierced the hull. The Russian tank shuddered then blew apart, somehow losing every roadwheel on the left side of the vehicle in the explosion so that when the smoke cleared the steel beast sagged down on one side like a sinking ship, spewing smoke and flames.

"Finish them off!" Wayland shouted into the comms like a cry to battle.

The two Abrams fired as they attacked. The T-90 commanders turned their turrets to face down the threat but had no time to maneuver. One tank fired a snap-shot that destroyed a nearby building but missed Wayland's tank entirely. A second gunner had more poise. He fired at Wayland's Abrams and struck the front left track. Wayland's tank lurched and then an almighty clamor of grinding noise screeched through the steel hull. The driver cried out that the vehicle had thrown a track. Wayland cursed bitterly but urged JJ to keep finding targets. Stranded, and unable to move, the tank was like a beached whale. His only hope was to fend off the enemy lest they circle like sharks to destroy him.

Sergeant McGrath saw Wayland's tank enveloped in smoke and heard the loud 'crack!' of a shot striking home. There were three more T-90s in sight. He targeted the closest enemy vehicle and ordered the gunner to fire.

The interior of Wayland's tank smelled of cordite and oil and sweat. The air was thick with a haze of dust. Another Russian tank fired at the Abrams and the round clanged off the turret's front armor. The noise inside the steel hull was huge as a tolling bell. Wayland targeted the tank and JJ fired. The shot struck the T-90 but deflected off the angled armor of the hull.

"Re-engage!"

JJ fired again. The second round caught the enemy tank broadside and blew through the engine compartment. The T-90 began to brew up. A turret hatch sprung open and a billow of smoke erupted from within. A man scrambled out through the cupola, dragging himself with his hands, his trailing legs paralyzed. His eyes were wide with terror. He fell to the ground in the long grass. His face was burned and his clothes smoldering. No one else escaped the ruin.

"Finish them off!" Sergeant McGrath's gunner fired at a T-90 crossing the football field, striking the tank in the rear where it most vulnerable. The tank exploded into a thousand pieces of fragmented metal.

The remaining Russian tanks fell back, firing smoke grenades as they reversed. Wayland's CITV monitor turned to a white blur as the thermal sights became blinded by the fierce flare. He cursed and gritted his teeth. Somewhere in the choking smoke McGrath's tank fired twice more and then suddenly the battlefield fell eerily silent.

Wayland kept staring at his onboard screens until the thermal flare cleared and he realized the enemy had retreated. He blinked sweat from his eyes and heaved in a deep breath. His hands were shaking. He bunched them into tight fists and swallowed a lump of fear that had lodged in his throat.

Across the Company net, Major Browne's Irish brogue sounded deceptively casual in the aftermath of the ferocious battle. "Grand work, Red Platoon. The enemy have legged it back to the north. You can return to the village. The party's over – for now."

Chapter 8:

A young Corporal sobbed and then cried out pitifully. His left arm was gone below the elbow, severed by a Russian howitzer shell. He pleaded for morphine; his face waxen and sweating. A medic consoled the soldier but the weeping went on through the night. The other wounded men lay groaning and retching. They were laid out along a corridor of the school building, the floor awash with smeared streaks of blood. A Sergeant, his face swathed in bandages, sat propped against a wall smoking quietly until he collapsed sideways and died.

Major Browne and Wayland walked amongst the injured. The stench in the long corridor was the mingled odors of fresh blood and vomit and sweating fear. A man who had been burned in a flash of fire stared blindly at the far wall. The flames had burned off his left ear, then melted the flesh of his cheek and his lips, exposing his teeth and his jaw bone. The putrid, sickly-sweet stench of roasted flesh pricked at Wayland's nostrils. The man looked like a survivor of some obscene holocaust. He would be dead before dawn.

"Eight more dead and twice as many wounded," Major Browne muttered gravely, surveying the long line of injured with a forlorn shrug of despair. "I've barely a platoon of fit men left. Plus, we lost another one of your tanks – "

"Two tanks," Wayland corrected. They reached the end of the corridor and went quietly out through the doors and into the twilight of dusk.

"Two?"

"Yes. My Abrams was struck on the track. No tank takes a hit like that from a 120mm sabot round at close range and emerges unscathed. Most of the roadwheels are mangled and so are the comp idler arms. Two of the ballistic side skirts were blown off their hinges, and the track is in a thousand pieces. It will have to be scuttled."

"Scuttled?" The Irish Major's frowned. The loss of two Abrams reduced the number of tanks at his disposal to six.

Wayland nodded. "We can't leave it for the enemy. There's a SOP for destroying an Abrams. The men are making the preparations now."

In 2003, an Abrams involved in the 'Thunder Run' – the armored push through the city of Baghdad – was disabled by an RPG. The decision was made to wreck the tank, but an Abrams is almost indestructible, and killing the vehicle had proved frustratingly troublesome. After another Abrams had fired on the stricken tank and been unable to destroy it, the Air Force were compelled to bomb the vehicle. Since that time, an SOP had been developed for scuttling an Abrams. It was a detailed procedure that required the tankers to remove the crew-served machine guns, and then 'zero' out the radios. Then the coax, 50cal and main tank ammunition was salvaged and shared amongst the remaining tanks. Two HEAT rounds were left on the turret floor and another in the driver's compartment to act as fire accelerants before the crew locked open all the main gun ammunition doors and manually activated the fire suppression system. Finally a crewman laid a thermite grenade on top of the breech block.

After dousing the turret and the inside of the tank with fuel and turbo shaft oil, more thermite grenades were thrown inside the turret and the driver's compartment. The subsequent cataclysmic explosion destroyed everything inside the vehicle and rendered it useless to the enemy.

Wayland finished explaining and made a helpless gesture with his hands.

"Six tanks and a handful of infantry won't be enough to hold off another Russian attack," Major Browne said bleakly.

"No," Wayland agreed.

They reached the street and began to walk towards the intersection. Nightfall was fast approaching. The smoke had thinned but still an eerie pall hung over the devastated village. Men moved quietly about, distributing ammunition and MREs. Two infantrymen sat side-by-side with their backs against a bullet-pocked concrete wall, sharing a cigarette. No one spoke much.

Wayland could not remember a fight so bitter, so intense. His previous combat experiences paled in comparison. In Afghanistan the terror had come from determined bands of insurgents. At the Battle of Jekabpils a few weeks earlier, he had been just a small part of a vast conflict. Here the fearful chaos was confined to a few square miles of ruined, blood-soaked village. Despair and despondency hung over the settlement, crushing morale.

"Any word from Command about our reinforcements?" Wayland asked without expectation.

"The French are still coming," Major Browne gave a thin wry smile. "They've reached the outskirts of Warsaw."

"We won't see them before noon tomorrow," Wayland guessed.

Major Browne nodded. "But I don't think the Ruskies will try a night attack. I think they've had quite enough for one day. My guess is that they'll wait for the rest of the Army to mass and then hit us at dawn."

"And in the meantime…?"

As if to answer the looming question, the far horizon lit up with a glow of red light and a moment later a howitzer shell whistled through the air. Wayland listened to the menacing sound approaching and instinctively seized the Irish Major's arm. "Get under shelter!"

They threw themselves down behind a crumbling brick wall and covered their heads with their hands.

The shell landed three hundred yards behind the school. Wayland felt the rumble of the explosion through the earth. The two men looked at each other. "It's going to be a long night."

Russian howitzer shells began to rain down on the village. One shell landed fifty yards from Sergeant McGrath's Abrams, and the vehicle rocked on its suspension from the proximity of the explosion. Another landed in the school's carpark, destroying an abandoned car. The next shell overshot and landed in the carpark of the hotel, several hundred yards behind the intersection. The American tankers climbed into their vehicles and closed the hatches to endure the nightmare. The Irish infantry cowered in the dubious shelter of whatever ruined buildings they could find. The shells turned the darkness into a horrid nightmare. Each howitzer fired independently, establishing its own particular rhythm. Sometimes the shells fell in pairs. At other times there was a gap of thirty seconds and then four shells would explode in unison. The shells landed with a 'crump!'. Fragments rattled through the leaves and frayed men's nerves. One explosion struck a rainwater tank at the rear of a house and it erupted like a crashing wave.

Wayland took command of Captain Kohn's tank at the intersection and brought his gunner, J.J Brown, with him to work with the Captain's loader and driver. He distributed his driver and Swanny into other vehicles until each of the remaining six Company tanks had a full crew.

He stared around the gloomy interior of Kohn's tank and was struck by the sense of familiarity. The Captain's Abrams had the same smells, the idling engine had the same sounds. Only a small wallet-sized photo taped to the bulkhead by the tank commander's seat seemed out of place. It was a photo of an older man with two younger uniformed soldiers. Wayland studied the image and guessed it was a picture of Kohn's hero father and his two step-brothers. He tore the photo down and threw it out through the turret hatch.

At midnight the howitzers suddenly stopped firing. Gradually, like men emerging from the aftermath of a mighty storm, the survivors throughout the village crept out from their shelters, coughing in the smoke and blinking in appalled dismay at the fresh devastation. Most of the narrow village streets were cratered and rubble-strewn. More buildings were on fire, the flames fanned by a stiffening breeze. The leaping fires painted the nightmare ruins in flickering lurid light. It was like a scene from Hell.

Some men made a feeble attempt to put out the flames but most just stared, numb and shell-shocked. Then the howitzers started up again and the air filled once more with the sounds of whistling death. The first shell struck the side of a house near the intersection. The front wall collapsed in a cloud of dust and debris. Men scattered. Someone shouted. A young soldier stumbled and was heaved to his feet by a comrade who dragged him to shelter.

Wayland abandoned his tank and went out into the night to find Major Browne.

*

Wayland found Major Browne and Captain O'Malley in the rubble of a house on the western outskirts of the village. The Irishmen were surveying the infantry's positions and peering out into the eerily still night. Overhead, a thick slice of moon hung low in the sky.

"We could put the American mortar carrier behind that wall," Captain O'Malley suggested, pointing. He raised his voice above the sound of a nearby howitzer shell exploding. "From there it could cover our front line of trenches and enfilade an enemy advance."

Major Browne nodded. The tank company's M106A3 mortar track was parked in the middle of the street. Relocating it to the end of the road would broaden its field of fire should the Russians launch a fresh attack across the fields in the morning.

Wayland reached the two men, sidestepping mounds of broken debris. Major Browne looked haggard, the strain deepening the chiselled lines of his face. He stood hunched in the thick folds of a long coat and although he was fatigued to the point at which his fingers and feet felt numb and his eyes as though they were filled with grit, yet no thought of sleep entered his mind. There was too much to plan, too many imponderables to factor. And he was afraid. A black pall of despair and hopelessness weighed down on him.

The Russians had very nearly cracked the fragile defence he had constructed several times already. It seemed as though nothing would stand in their way at sunrise.

He also feared for the safety of his remaining men, and those already wounded should the Russians overwhelm the village outskirts before the injured troops could be evacuated. The enemy might seek ruthless vengeance for the heavy toll of casualties they had suffered. It would not be the first time a siege had ended in wholesale savage slaughter.

"I had a couple of ideas," Wayland began, drawing the Irish officer from the depths of his dark torment.

Major Browne roused himself and arched his eyebrow. "I'm listening."

"First, I think we should send out a recce mission; two men going north in the night to give us eyes on the enemy so we can have a better understanding of what we'll be up against at sunrise. Your drones don't have the range, and they're only effective in daylight conditions. And if we wait until morning it will be too late. But if we can see the shape of the enemy and get a sense from where they're likely to launch their next attack early enough, we might be able to reposition ourselves."

The two Irishmen exchanged glances and a wry smile.

"I've just been discussing the same idea with Captain O'Malley here. He has volunteered for the mission," the Major said.

Wayland blinked. "When?"

"Thirty minutes from now. He's taking one of our Sergeants with him – a good man."

"Recce only?"

"Yes. Of course. Two men can't take on the entire Russian Army, and I doubt a prisoner will be able to tell us anything useful – unless he's a bloody General. So, yes, Lieutenant. The Captain has orders to observe and report back only."

Wayland nodded and felt a small lift of relief. Information was the most powerful weapon of warfare. Knowing where the enemy was and what they were planning might save lives, and perhaps, temporarily, save the village. He glanced apprehensively north one final time and saw a faint glow of light emanating from beyond the low dark skyline.

"And your second idea?" Major Browne prompted. A Russian howitzer shell struck an abandoned car on the far side of the street and all three men ducked their heads instinctively.

"The mother of all IED's," Wayland said. "Planted on the shoulder of the road by the intersection. Six mortar shells, all wired to a detonator that could be activated by a hand-held radio."

Major Browne gave a foxy smile and his eyes turned cunning. "You fight dirty, Lieutenant."

"It's a dirty war, Major," Wayland made no apologies.

"Permission granted."

*

Major Browne walked with Captain O'Malley and Sergeant Sweeney to the outskirts of the village and sent them on their way into the night. The men's faces and hands had been blackened. They carried just a radio, their personal L85 rifles, and a handful of grenades in the event of an emergency. They carried no packs, no food or water, only spare ammunition.

The Major watched the two men set out into the farm fields, moving like wraiths, until the darkness swallowed them up, then turned and walked back along the street, stopping to talk with weary men who stood their post, and to pass around cigarettes.

Captain O'Malley set a brisk pace, using the hedgerows, ruined BMP-3 wreckage, and clumps of furrowed ground for cover. When they reached the bottom of the rise, O'Malley crouched low behind a clump of bushes and checked his watch. Thirty minutes had elapsed since they had left the village. He pulled Sergeant Sweeney down close to him. The Captain was sweating lightly, cautious and nervous. Somewhere in the distance he could hear the heavy rumble and clatter of tracked vehicles on the move. The vibration came up through the soles of his boots.

"There is a grove of trees on the skyline. That's where we will reconnoitre from."

The Sergeant nodded.

O'Malley led the way, moving in stalking fits and starts, crouched low. The sky was lighter than the landscape, and he feared silhouetting himself as he reached the crest. Sergeant Sweeney followed in the Captain's shadow, the two men moving noiselessly in the night until the ground underfoot began to level off as the gentle crest approached.

They were fifty paces too far to the left. O'Malley cursed under his breath and crabbed sideways, crawling the last ten paces through the long grass. The earth beneath his chest was corrugated as though this land long ago had been under the plough. He reached the stand of trees that loomed like a hulking shadow, blocking out the sliver of moonlight, and paused to steady his breath and settle his jangling nerves. Somewhere nearby on the air he could smell cigarette smoke mingled with the heavier, thicker stench of diesel fumes. He felt Sergeant Sweeney tug gently on his left boot; the signal that he was in position and ready to move again.

Captain O'Malley came up into a crouch and ghosted into the fringe of trees. A conflicting brew of emotions overwhelmed him. He was grateful for the cover; he had felt exposed in the open fields. But now he felt vulnerable to the threat of unseen danger lurking nearby.

He crept through the tall trees, lifting his feet and placing them down gently to avoid the crack of a snapping branch or the scuff of dead leaves. The air was rich with the odors of mossy, earthy undergrowth. He felt his heart begin to race. He blinked sweat from his eyes and then froze as the sound of a throaty voice sliced across the fraught silence of the night.

"Day mne sigaretu."

Captain O'Malley's heart skipped a beat and a trickle of chilled sweat ran down his back. He held his breath and, without turning his head or moving a muscle, swivelled his eyes towards the sound.

He peered hard into the inky blackness, straining. He saw nothing – until a thin blue feather of smoke rose through the trees, and a moment later the pungent aroma of tobacco tarnished the air. O'Malley blinked and gradually the outline of a man came into focus. He sat, partly obscured by a snarl of foliage, about twenty paces away with his back against a tree. The Irish Captain kept staring until the shape of the man emerged. Then he saw another figure nearby. The second man was squatting over something on the ground. He finished with the object and rose to his feet with a weary groan.

O'Malley cursed under his breath. He guessed the Russians were the two-man crew of an OP, set forward, somewhere closer to the crest of the rise from where they could observe the village. For long seconds he did not move, weighing his options. He could ghost around the Russians, but the fear of being discovered on their way back to the village haunted him. His only other choice was to kill the two enemy soldiers and hope their deaths were not noticed. If they were required to contact command at regular intervals, a search party would be sent to discover the reason for their missed check-in. All hell would break loose when the bodies were discovered.

Captain O'Malley made his decision. He turned in slow motion until he had eye contact with Sergeant Sweeney. He made small signals with his hands. The big Irish Sergeant understood. The men separated, moving with exaggerated caution in the night until they were in position.

The two Russians were making idle desultory talk, sharing cigarettes between them. One of the soldiers got to his feet and unbuttoned his fly. He turned and took half-a-dozen steps into the nearby trees – and then cried out in a strangled gasp of alarm as Sergeant Sweeney wrapped his huge hands around the Russian's throat and twisted savagely. The sound of his neck breaking was like the sudden snap of a tree branch. He fell dead to the ground with a thud. It was Captain O'Malley's signal to strike. He launched himself out of the dark at the second man and the two figures rolled across the small clearing of ground. O'Malley had surprise and impetus. He pinned the

Russian on his back and covered the man's gaping mouth with the palm of his hand. He fumbled in the dirt, and his fist wrapped around a baseball-sized rock. He clubbed the Russian to death, raising the rock over his head again and again and smashing it down into the soldier's face until he could feel nothing but bloody mushed pulp beneath his sticky fingers.

He rolled off the corpse, breathing hard, his lungs heaving like a bellows. His hands were awash with the Russian's blood. Sergeant Sweeney dragged the two bodies deeper into the undergrowth.

The Irishmen moved on into the night, their steps now more urgent. They reached the northern fringe of the grove and dropped to the ground, crawling forward until they had a sweeping moonlit view of the vast depression of land that lay before them.

The valley itself appeared to be fields of crops, beaten flat by the tracks of hundreds of heavy vehicles. Patches of ground glowed dully under the moon's glow. Then suddenly and incredibly, an army began to emerge from the darkened shadows as Captain O'Malley's eyes adjusted to the silvery light.

The Russians were spread out in an arrogant display of might and power.

Silhouettes of T-90s, APCs and trucks began to emerge, arranged in orderly parked phalanxes with the transport trucks far to the rear by the edge of a dense forest. Ahead of them stood a long row of field artillery and nearer to the road from Lomza were parked lines of mobile artillery. Closer to where the Captain lay were rank upon rank of BMPs, some with their slitted lights glowing and their engines trailing diesel exhaust into the night sky. The Irish Captain gaped. He had never seen such an array of overwhelming military strength. It remined him of the old Soviet Victory Day parades that he had seen broadcast on television, marching through Red Square under the stern gaze of the Soviet leadership.

Sergeant Sweeney studied the awesome menace of the arrayed Russian Army for several long seconds and then asked in a whisper, "Where are all their tanks, sir?"

Captain O'Malley frowned and studied the scene in the valley more carefully. He could make out the shape of T-90s and perhaps old T-72s lined in ranks by the side of the road with their lights ablaze… but he realised the force seemed dramatically unbalanced. It was heavy in artillery and APCs, yet in proportion he could see very few Russian tanks. His frown deepened and something unsettling and ominous slithered in the pit of his guts.

"Perhaps they're still on the road, still yet to arrive…" he took a feeble guess and then crawled backwards until he was within the sheltered shadows of the grove. When both men were in cover, the Captain sprang urgently to his feet. "I've seen enough. We've got to get back to the village and warn Major Browne about what's coming to kill us in the morning."

*

The Irish dead, wrapped within black body bags, were being respectfully loaded onto the flatbed of a transport truck behind the school building when Captain O'Malley returned to Stare Lubiejewo. He looked like the hideous apparition from a nightmare. His hands and uniform were stained with spattered blood and dirt, his face a gruesome grimy mask, streaked with runnels of sweat. He burst into the ground floor classroom where Wayland and Major Browne were waiting. It was three-thirty in the morning. No one had slept for days. The Major and the American Lieutenant looked haggard and bleak.

O'Malley saluted. Major Browne flinched, aghast. He seemed to shudder in reaction to the man's gruesome appearance. "Are you injured, Captain?"

"No, sir," O'Malley brushed ineffectually at the blood stains. "It's not my blood, sir. It's Russian."

Wayland and the Major exchanged meaningful glances. Major Browne beckoned the Captain into the room. "Well, what did you see?"

"Sergeant Sweeney and I reconnoitred the enemy position from the dense grove of trees on the skyline. The Russians are arrayed in the valley beyond; hundreds of APCs and rows of field artillery. They also have at least a company of mobile artillery close to the northern road." On an impulse he went to the classroom blackboard and began drawing the enemy's dispositions. He swayed on his feet with fatigue.

"Tanks?" Wayland wanted to know.

Captain O'Malley licked dry cracked lips. "I saw T-90s and they might have some old T-72s as well. They're formed up close to the road ahead of the mobile artillery," he drew their position onto the blackboard. "But…"

"But what?" Major Browne asked curtly, frowning.

"But there doesn't seem to be enough heavy armor to balance the force, sir," Captain O'Malley seemed exasperated. "And I can't, for the life of me, understand why."

"Maybe the remainder of the force's tanks are still on the road, traveling," Wayland speculated.

"Yes," the Captain seemed unconvinced. "That's what I initially thought too. But an army doesn't advance with transport trucks and artillery, Lieutenant. Armor always leads the way…"

"So, where the bloody hell are the rest of the Russian tanks?" Major Browne puzzled. "And what will it mean for us in the morning?"

Wayland got to his feet and stretched stiffened muscles. He yawned, exhausted. "Your recce mission seems to have thrown up more questions than answers, Captain," he observed ominously. His eyes felt impossibly heavy, yet he knew there would be no sleep again this night.

Captain O'Malley said nothing.

Major Browne drew a deep breath and sighed like a condemned man on his way to the gallows to meet an inevitable fate. "In the morning the Russians will come and we will fight them wherever they appear, no matter how determined they are. We stand our ground because we've been ordered to hold the bastards up for as long as possible, and until I get orders otherwise that's what we will continue to do."

A quote from Milton came to the Irish officer's mind unbidden, and he whispered the words into the quiet room, for the sentiment seemed to sum up the hopeless futility of their situation.

"Where no hope is left, is left no fear."

Chapter 9:

There were no loud noises to rouse the men, nothing that would disturb the fragile pre-dawn silence. The Sergeants shook the soldiers awake, and they came alert cursing softly and wheezing from the lingering smoke that caught deep in their lungs. Every man's first reaction was to glance north towards the darkened skyline, but the world was very still. The distant rise showed merely as a softly silhouetted line under the fading moonlight.

Some of the Irishmen brewed tea. The American tankers strung pots filled with water from lengths of rope and left them dangling against the tank's engine exhaust to boil. The men were hollow-cheeked and haggard, their faces unshaven, their uniforms filthy and torn, some stained with blood. Sunrise was still an hour away. They groped in the gloomy pre-dawn and cleaned their weapons with the fanaticism of men who knew their lives depended on their efficient working order.

Major Browne started his inspection chatting briefly to the handful of lightly injured men at the eastern end of the village. One had his hand wrapped in a swathe of bandages. Another limped, favouring his right leg. There were six men in total. The Major accepted a tin mug of scalding tea from a Corporal and reassured the soldiers that a French relief column was expected within a few hours. The Major turned towards the horizon, still cradling the mug in his hands, and stared at the impenetrable wall of the great forest that protected the flank. It was a shade darker than the land and several shades darker than the lightening sky, ominous and silent and somehow menacing. He cast aside his foreboding and flashed the injured a wry smile. "Who would have thought it, lads?" he swept his eyes around the faces of the men. They were scared and suffering. "The bloody French are coming to save us."

They shared a hollow half-hearted laugh, but the sound was strained with tension. Major Browne handed back the mug of unfinished tea to the Corporal and sauntered west like he was taking a carefree stroll. He reached a knot of soldiers around the bombed ruins of the intersection. There were two

Javelin teams posted amongst the grey dusty rubble. His boots crunched over broken bricks and warned the men he was coming.

"All quiet?"

"Aye, sir."

The eastern skyline at last began to show the first hints of colour, a smear of pale grey light that deepened the silhouette of the great forest and defined the line of the rise to the north. Major Browne sat with one of the Javelin crews and handed out cigarettes. The two men looked young and anxious. Their fresh-faced complexions were smeared with dusty grime, streaked with runnels of sweat. In the corner of the ditch sat the Javelin CLU and the crew's three remaining missiles, stacked in their long black transport tubes. The Javelin team were intimidated by the presence of their commanding officer. Finally, one of the men cleared his throat and asked in a quiet voice, "Will it be bad today, sir?"

Major Browne smiled and assured the young soldier the coming Russian attack would not be as terrifying as he feared, then clapped the man on the shoulder. "Just follow your training and you'll be fine."

He left the narrow trench and reached the intersection. Wayland was standing in the gloom. From somewhere far away a dog barked and then a rooster crowed. Wayland stood staring at the shoulder of the road where, during the night, the massive IED had been buried. The site had been concealed beneath handfuls of scattered debris and dead leaves so that it matched the surrounding ground perfectly. He wondered idly if the device would explode when triggered.

"Anything?"

Wayland shook his head. "Not a sound."

The Major checked his watch. Sunrise was thirty minutes away. The handful of men on picquet duty were relieved, and the Irish infantry roused themselves and stood to their posts. The air seemed to crackle with anxious tension.

Dawn crept slowly over the vast mass of forest, spilling soft grey light across the village and surrounding fields. Storm clouds the color of old bruises and heavy with the rain they carried swept in from the north, diffusing the morning light and casting the landscape in a dull ominous mist.

Wayland walked back to his tank. His crew were drinking the last of the coffee. J.J handed Wayland a tin mug. The men looked worn down by the relentless strain of the past eighteen hours. Major Browne strolled west to the end of the village where the last of his three surviving Javelin crews were posted.

The two-man team had been positioned in the second-floor ruins of a bombed house, close to the American tank company's mortar carrier. One of the Irishmen was standing in the ground floor doorway of the ruin, exchanging MREs and a mug of coffee with an American mortar crewman. The Irishman saw Major Browne approaching and stiffened guiltily. The officer waved the man's salute away.

"Coffee, O'Leary?" he took the tin mug and sipped the scalding contents. "What would your dear mother say if she knew her young lad had given up tea in favor of this swill?"

The young Irish soldier grinned. "Sorry, sir."

Major Browne gave a disarming smile. "I shall pray for your soul, Private, in the hope that God will forgive you."

The Major handed back the mug and walked on until he was at the very edge of the village, from where, just a few hours earlier, he had sent Captain O'Malley and Sergeant Sweeney on their way into the night. The morning was eerily silent.

An hour after sunrise, the Russians still had not come. A light drizzle began to fall. The rain glistened in the grass-flattened fields and turned the dusty rubble of the village to mud. Thunder rumbled across the sky and a flash of lightning flickered.

Two hours after sunrise distant machine gun fire could be heard, coming from the valley beyond the skyline. The soldiers came alert with sudden alarm and cocked their ears. A soldier in his trench turned and looked a worried question at Major Browne. The officer shook his head and said in a voice loud enough for all the men defending the western flank of the village to hear.

"Machine gun fire ain't going to herald an enemy attack, lads. Nothing's going to happen until their howitzers open fire."

At nine o'clock a small knot of Russian officers appeared on the gentle slope of the distant crest. Major Browne studied the enemy through his binoculars. A tall solidly-built man in a long woollen coat stood at the head of the gathering, surrounded by a dozen aides and junior officers. Captain O'Malley appeared at the Major's side and looked north.

"They're taking their time," O'Malley muttered.

"Yes," Major Browne set aside the binoculars. "But why? What in God's name are they waiting for?"

"More tanks?"

The Major grunted. He glanced at his watch and shook his head. "It's a quarter after the hour. Maybe they don't know there is a French column on its way from Warsaw to relieve us. Maybe their intelligence satellites are not functioning. They might think they have all the armor, the men and the time they need just to roll up to the village and crush us whenever they feel like it."

"Maybe," Captain O'Malley muttered defiantly. "But if that's what they believe, they're in for one hell of a surprise and one hell of a fight, sir."

Two minutes later the first enemy howitzer shell whistled through the air and exploded south of the intersection.

The waiting was over.

The Russians, at last, were attacking.

*

A howitzer shell landed on the southeastern edge of the village, two streets behind the main intersection. The shell struck a brick wall surrounding a small church, knocking down cemetery headstones, hurling a debris of rubble fragments into the air, and shattering several of the old building's stained-glass windows. Another Russian shell landed in the nearby narrow street, exploding a flat-bed farm truck stacked with bales of hay. Flames leaped high into the sky and spread to nearby abandoned houses. Soon half the buildings along the narrow street were on fire. The pall of smoke mingled with the heavy canopy of storm clouds.

The barrage continued, growing in snarling ferocity until it seemed the air was thick with the whistling whine of incoming shells. The beleaguered survivors defending the village cowered in their trenches as the earth around them leaped and shuddered.

Some men silently prayed, their mouths moving over the invocations until they became a kind of chant. Other men clamped their hands over their heads and closed their eyes as clods of dirt rained down on their backs. The thunderous 'crump!' of each explosion mingled together until they seemed endless. The air quivered. The percussion of the heavy howitzer shells detonating felt like a physical blow. The air thickened and grew hotter until each gasping breath seemed to sear the lungs. It was like standing at the doors of a vast flaming furnace.

Two howitzer shells landed a split-second apart on a decrepit mechanics workshop in a side lane and obliterated it. Wayland and his crew scrambled into their tank. Wayland remained standing upright in the turret. The farm fields were shrouded in drifting smoke, illuminated by the flare of light from Russian artillery batteries behind the skyline each time they fired. The flashes glimmered against the belly of the low thunder clouds so that it looked like the distant sky was filled with flickers of lightning.

Wayland could see no signs of an enemy armored attack. The smoke shroud across the village thickened so that for a disconcerting moment he had the impression that he was the only living soul left on the battlefield.

Then he heard the ominous clunk and rattle of steel tracks and the far-away growl of heavy revving engines. Through the smoke that blanketed the western fields he saw dark shapes moving; at least a dozen BMP-3s dashing forward in loose order. He broke across the Company net to shout a warning. "Enemy PC's advancing on the skyline!"

The men defending the outskirts readied themselves. The Javelin team on the second floor of the bomb-ruined building sighted their first target as the Russian armored personnel carriers reached the furthest hedgerow, still over a thousand yards away. The operator locked on to the BMP-3 and launched.

The Javelin missile leaped from the weapon's control unit and blasted skyward, autonomously guided to the target. It climbed to a height of one hundred and fifty meters and then plunged down like a swooping hawk. The missile hit the flimsy top armor of the Russian troop carrier and blew the vehicle into a million ragged steel fragments, slaughtering the three man crew and the nine enemy infantry contained inside instantly. The impact of the huge explosion blew both tracks off the BMP-3's hull so all that remained was a twisted carcass of mangled steel beneath a towering column of boiling smoke.

Major Brown watched the Russian troop carrier explode from atop the school building's roof. He snatched for his radio and his voice was loud and frantic through the static.

"Hit those PC's early. Don't wait for them to close. Take them out before they can unload their infantry!"

Only two Abrams now defended the western flank of the village, with Wayland's tank and one other guarding the crossroad against another T-90 attack down the road. Wayland had left a single Abrams to protect the eastern side of the settlement and kept McGrath's Abrams behind the school as a ready reserve. They were stretched too thin. The enemy were overwhelming.

The two Abrams to the west of his position opened fire with HEAT rounds. The vehicles were hull-down amongst rubble. Wayland saw the twin flashes as each Abrams fired and a second later two more BMP-3s exploded in flames and roiling smoke. Then the building that concealed the closest

Abrams blew apart. Rubble and debris collapsed down on the tank.

Wayland peered hard along the smoke-hazed skyline. "Enemy tanks, hull-down behind the rise. They're covering the advance."

"Ignore them Red One," Major Browne barked. "All units, ignore the Russian tanks. Keep firing on the PC's. They must be stopped before their infantry can unload and overwhelm us." It was the Major's greatest fear; a wave of Russian infantry reaching the outskirt buildings and overpowering the handful of defenders by sheer weight of numbers.

Wayland dropped down into the turret and pulled his hatch closed behind him. In truth, the risk of a hull-down Abrams being destroyed by a T-90 from over two thousand yards was slim. But the presence of the tanks on the skyline proved an ominous change of tactics from the enemy. Until this moment, their attempts to seize the village had been one-dimensional. Now artillery, armor and APCs were working together in the way that modern warfare was meant to be fought.

Wayland peered through his tank's CITV and saw a BMP-3 through his thermal sights. The vehicle was at the second line of hedgerows, slowing to batter its way through the wall of dense bushes. He thumbed the button on his commander's override handle. The tank's turret swung onto its target.

"Designate PC! Load HEAT!"

"Up!" Captain Kohn's loader barked in a voice so loud with tension that it startled Wayland. He was a small wiry man from Ruidoso, New Mexico, with dark eyes and a suntanned complexion.

"Identified!" Gunner J.J. Brown engaged the target and centered the sight reticle. He stabbed the laser button with his thumb. The range was eight hundred yards. The Abram's fire control system performed its electronic witchcraft, calculating air density and humidity.

"Fire and adjust!" Wayland gave the command.

J.J. thumbed the trigger. "On the way!"

The Abrams rocked with the recoil of the shot and the round leaped from the barrel at supersonic speed, trailing a dragon's breath of flame. A heartbeat later the enemy vehicle blew apart. The sound of the shattering explosion carried across the battlefield.

"Target!" J.J declared.

Wayland's sudden APC kill was observed from the skyline and drew savage retribution. Two of the T-90s fired on the crossroad. Both shots missed Wayland's tank, but struck close enough to shake the seventy-ton steel beast on its suspension and collapse a nearby wall.

The enemy howitzers fired a final, furious salvo and then fell suddenly silent as the closest surviving BMP-3s closed within five hundred yards of the village. A hail of suppressing fire from machine guns mounted on the troop carriers replaced the numbing barrage of howitzer shells. An Irish infantryman was struck in the midriff by a flurry of bullets and cried out. He had been hunched behind the crumbled brick foundations of a bomb-ruined home. He was flung down by the impact of the fusillade and fell screaming. Trailing a wet smear of blood behind him, he tried to crawl for help, but died instead.

The heavens opened and the air filled with a sudden deluge of rain. The farm fields became veiled in a grey impenetrable mist. The Russian APCs reached the final line of hedgerows, and their rear doors opened. Armed infantry burst out into the torrential downpour, their heavy boots sloshing in the mud. The enemy were shouting; Wayland could see their mouths moving but the sound of their cheers and screams were drowned out by distance and the fury of machine gun fire. An Irish Sergeant pointed out targets to his men. "Fire!"

Troops in the vanguard of the enemy attack went down in the firefight, clutching at gruesome wounds and sobbing with pain. But still the enemy came stolidly on. A Russian Lieutenant put a whistle to his mouth and blew three shrill notes. The infantry on the ground around him sprang bravely to their feet and dashed forward. The staccato roar of the

Russian heavy machine guns took on the tempo of pounding drums, seeming to beat the advance. Three Irish soldiers rose from their trench and opened fire. The Russian Lieutenant died, his blood spattered against the hull of an APC. The small attack faltered and then faded into fresh gore and screams.

Then, from the crest of the rise, another dozen enemy APCs appeared. They came surging down the gentle slope towards the village, their tracks flailing mud and grass in their wake.

The second wave of the attack dashed forward almost unmolested. The American tanks were overwhelmed with closer targets. Wayland locked on to an APC behind the nearest hedgerow and J.J engaged.

The vehicle was spraying the outlying buildings of the village with its mounted heavy machine gun to suppress counter-fire while the nine infantrymen it carried spilled out through the rear doors into the muddy field. The shot from the Abrams struck the BMP-3 almost broadside. The wicked impact of the strike blew the Russian vehicle into the air and flipped it over, killing the crew and most of the infantrymen in a deadly hail of steel fragments. Only two enemy soldiers survived the APC's destruction. One man had been struck in the face. He fell to the ground screaming and clutching at his wounds. The second wounded soldier tried doggedly to claw his way forward even though his entrails spilled out from a slashing gut wound. He drowned face-down in a puddle of red-stained mud.

The Abrams' defending the western flank destroyed three more enemy troop carriers beyond the near hedgerow before the second wave of BMP-3s arrived to reinforce the assault. The Irish infantry entrenched closest to the enemy fired one last final time and fell back to new defensive positions across the street. The Russian infantry swarmed out of their transports like angry ants from a disturbed nest and went to ground, firing and moving, firing and moving.

Wayland could sense the Irish were on the verge of being overwhelmed. One man lay dead in the street, face down in a waterlogged shell crater. He had been shot in the back as he had broken cover.

"White Two and Three, advance!" Wayland rolled the dice on a desperate gamble. "Close and engage the enemy PC's and troops!"

The two tanks broke free of the rubble that sheltered them and dashed gamely out into the fields, firing from point-blank range at the enemy troop carriers. A handful of advancing Russian infantry were crushed under their surging steel tracks. Others were scythed down by the Abrams' machine guns. Three BMP-3s exploded in quick succession before the first of the enemy APCs slewed round on its spinning steel tracks and began to edge backwards. With the Abrams' so close to their own troop carriers, the T-90s on the ridge fell silent, fearful of hitting friendly targets. One of the BMP-3s fired its main gun at an Abrams as it rampaged towards the hedgerow. The round struck the American tank's turret and deflected away harmlessly. Two more APCs fired at the same tank but the Abrams emerged, its sloped steel armor scorched and dented, but intact. The Russian infantry in the fields around the village lost all cohesion; they became just a cluster of desperate men who realized salvation depended on them retreating to the shelter of their troop carriers before the vehicles reversed and fled the field. The soldiers edged backwards, still firing to cover their withdrawal, and glanced nervously over their shoulders, fearful they would be abandoned.

Sensing the Russians were on the verge of buckling, the Irish infantry dashed forward once more to reclaim their abandoned firing positions. "Now, hit the bastards hard!" Sergeant Sweeney cried out, caught up in the madness and terrifying chaos. "Drive 'em back lads!"

The rain intensified into a drumming deluge. The roar of the firefight intensified. The battlefield became a mayhem of screams and chattering gunfire. The Russian infantry rose to their feet to flee and were felled like slaughtered cattle.

From the rooftop of the school building Major Browne felt a sudden exhausted lift of relief. The enemy were falling back.

He gave a hoarse cheer of exultation and heaved a long desperate sigh.

At which point the real Russian attack burst from the wall of dense forest that sheltered the eastern flank of Stare Lubiejewo.

*

A unit of Russian engineers had toiled for eleven hours to plot and clear a narrow trail through the great forest. They had worked non-stop throughout the night. Behind the engineers trundled a full company of T-72 tanks; ten Cold War era steel beasts that had been chosen for the initial attack because of their lightweight design and small size compared to their twenty-first century counterparts. Waiting beyond the northern fringe of the woods was another full Battalion of tanks, poised to exploit the initial breach once the route was mapped.

The tank Company at the tip of the Russian spear was led by Captain Pytor Bortnikov, a young dedicated officer eager for advancement. He was tasked with attacking the village's eastern outskirts once the defenders had been fully engaged by a feint assault from the west. Originally the plan had called for a dawn attack, but the engineers had encountered a dense grove of close-standing trees across their path that necessitated a dog-leg detour to southeast. As the sun rose across the rural Polish landscape, Bortnikov's tanks were still far from the fringe of the forest.

The diversionary assault was delayed and it was nine o'clock in the morning before the T-72s finally reached their jump-off point, a hundred meters inside the edge of the forest. Captain Bortnikov called a halt to the unwieldly column and dismounted his vehicle. Moving quickly through the woods he reached the margin of the forest and peered through high-powered binoculars at the village that lay a thousand yards away across an undulating field of wheat.

Stare Lubiejewo was under fire from howitzers that pounded the enemy's positions and filled the sky with a thunder of sound to conceal his column's advance. Much of the settlement appeared on fire; he could see several buildings ablaze beneath an ugly black scar of drifting smoke.

He strode purposefully back to his command vehicle and radioed headquarters. Ten minutes later the first wave of BMP-3s crested the skyline to the west of the village.

The thousand yards of open fields that separated the margin of the forest from the outskirts of the village's eastern edge worried the young Captain. He was aware that his T-72s were no match for the powerful American Abrams unless he could engage the enemy at close range and attack the bigger tank's vulnerable rear armor. Yet for his plan to work, first the enemy Abrams' must be drawn towards the far side of the village – and for that to happen, the troops in the BMP-3s must be sacrificed.

Bortnikov watched the first wave of APCs dash across the open farm fields, his view obscured by smoke and trees. He looked on anxiously. He wanted the BMP-3s to reach the outskirts of the village and for the infantry to dash into the first line of buildings… before being thrown back in disarray. He was not disloyal; he was ambitious. He saw this morning's attack as an opportunity to make a reputation for himself – to return victorious and be hailed as a valiant hero. He craved the glory and adulation. If the attack to the west of the village succeeded, his opportunity for fame would be snatched cruelly from him.

"Command is on the radio, sir," a junior officer saluted stiffly.

Bortnikov set aside his binoculars. "What do they want?"

"Colonel Pugacheva has ordered you to launch the attack immediately."

Bortnikov grunted but did not move. "Has the second wave of APCs been launched at the western flank?"

"They are cresting the rise as we speak."

"Then we wait," the young Captain lifted his chin arrogantly. "But tell the crews to mount up and battle carry sabot. When I give the order, they must be ready to advance at a moment's notice."

The officer saluted, turned on his heel and scampered back into the trees. Bortnikov spent another indulgent minute standing at the fringe of the woods. He glimpsed the second wave of APCs reach a line of hedges five hundred yards from the village and knew, by the ferocious sound of tank fire coming from within the village perimeter, that it was as far as the troop carriers would get.

In a matter of minutes, the attack would lose momentum. His time was now. This was the moment he had waited for.

He marched back to his tank. His vehicle was the fourth in line. He slammed the turret hatch closed behind him and spoke across the Company's radio network.

"Zaraneye!"

The tanks exploded from the fringe of the great forest in single file, driving like an arrow for the distant silhouette of the village. Once all ten T-72s were in the open wheat fields they maneuvered neatly into echelon, engines screaming as they charged to glory. Bortnikov dared to believe their attack had gone unnoticed. They closed to within five hundred yards of the village and still they had not been engaged by enemy fire. He felt the first tentative thrill of exultant anticipation and he shouted on the radio to urge his Company on.

"Faster! We are bound for glory. Victory is just a few hundred yards away!"

He had done it. He had launched a surprise attack and caught the vaunted American tanks off guard. In an hour the fight for the village would be won, and he would have a medal on his chest and the adulation of a grateful nation.

*

The handful of wounded Irish soldiers protecting the village's eastern outskirts were huddled together in a single house that stood at the end of a lane. They watched the Russian attack from the west through binoculars. They could not see the fighting clearly from their obscured location, but they could judge the intensity of the battle by the billowing smoke that stained the sky, and the cauldron of clamoring noise that grew in intensity with every passing second until the crackle of automatic fire and the heavy retort of tanks shooting melded into a single thunderous cacophony. A sergeant who had been shot in the shoulder and carried his injured arm in a sling handed the binoculars to anther wounded man and shook his head. "They're having a hard time of it, lads."

He fetched a tin mug and filled it with the last of the brewed tea, then idly glanced out through the kitchen window.

"Sweet weeping Jesus!" he gasped. "The feckin Russians are attacking us!" He threw down the mug and dived for the radio, cursing the pain of his wound as he fumbled with one hand. "Company Command, this is Eastern OP. Russian armor attacking in echelon from out of the forest! Repeat! At least a Company of enemy tanks attacking from out of the forest!"

Major Browne overheard the radio message and felt the blood drain from his face. He recoiled in numbed shock, then dashed to the corner of the school building's roof and peered through binoculars. A sickening nausea of dread slithered along his spine and crawled across the skin of his chest. For a moment he could not breathe.

The Irishman did not need the binoculars. Ten Russian T-72s were ploughing through wheat fields, driving for the eastern edge of the village. He could see the trail of crushed grain each vehicle left in its wake and the high haze of dust that billowed from beneath their tracks.

"White Four! White Four! Ten enemy T-72s your sector! Engage immediately!"

The one Abrams delegated to defending the village east of the intersection was parked between two houses a few hundred yards north of the school building. The commander ordered his driver to steer hard right and advance. The Abrams crashed through a wooden fence, its turbine engine howling.

"Red Four!" Major Browne's voice was loud and urgent in Sergeant McGrath's CVC headset. "Enemy tanks emerging from the eastern forest. Engage!"

McGrath's tank was parked amongst trees behind the school building, facing the intersection. He snarled at his driver. "Turn around! Get us in the fight!"

The two Abrams converged on the eastern outskirts, arriving at the network of narrow laneways sprinkled with cottages and farm buildings at high speed. By the time they were in position the Russian T-72s had crossed the wheat field and were amongst the outlying farmhouses.

The Abrams' advantage against the outdated Russian T-72 tanks was its superior armor and firepower. In a duel over long ranges across open ground, the Abrams was unbeatable. But in a street fight at close range those critical benefits were negated. Sergeant McGrath saw an enemy tank skirt behind the side of a barn and narrowed his eyes. The vehicle disappeared for a heartbeat and then emerged into the open, belching blue exhaust, its turret turning. The tank was mottled in green and brown camouflage, the front hull covered with an armadillo's skin of composite armor blocks.

"Designate Tank! Load sabot!"

"Up!" the loader barked.

"Identified!" the tank's gunner engaged the target. The range was just three hundred yards.

"Fire and adjust!" McGrath gave the command.

The gunner crushed the trigger and the Abrams flinched with the sudden recoil. "On the way!"

The T-72 was struck front-on, the impact of the sabot round so violent that it decapitated the tank, tearing off the turret and hurling it into the sky. The T-72 erupted in black oily smoke. A moment later flames leaped from the mangled hull.

"Target!" the gunner cheered.

McGrath hunted for a new enemy. The battlefield around the outlying buildings became shrouded in smoke and confusion. He caught a glimpse of two enemy tanks moving along a lane that would bring them around behind his position. McGrath ordered his driver to make a sharp turn and dashed to intercept.

The three T-72s burst through a fence and surged towards the main intersection. McGrath's gunner fired a snapshot that destroyed the lead tank, obliterating the left side roadwheels and shattering the steel track into mangled pieces. The other two Russian tanks were hemmed in by the ruined vehicle ahead of them and buildings on both sides of the street. They fired at McGrath's Abrams. Both shots struck the American tank from close range.

Whang! The first round clanged off the turret, scorching and creasing the armor but not penetrating. The second tank's sabot round deflected off the front hull. McGrath's gunner fired at the nearest T-72, and the tank blew apart into a million tiny steel fragments. The second Russian tank tried to reverse into a narrow side street but sideswiped the corner of a house. The wall collapsed onto the vehicle, covering it in dust and debris. McGrath's gunner put a sabot round through the hull, killing every man inside. Flames erupted from the punctured hulk and then, a moment later, the turret blew off the tank.

White Four accounted for two more of the T-72s, destroying the first enemy vehicle as it crashed through a mound of stacked firewood, and in the process killing Captain Bortnikov and ending his hopes of glory in a fireball of flames and steel fragments. The second T-72 rounded a tight corner and came up on the Abrams' rear like a cat stalking a mouse. As Bortnikov's tank blew apart, the second T-72 fired on White Four, targeting the flimsy stern armor. The sabot round tore into the engine block, crippling the vehicle. The Abrams turret turned and fired a last defiant time, destroying the T-72.

The crew abandoned the American tank, and dashed towards a nearby building, one of the men nursing a shattered arm and screaming in pain. The chattering fire of a Russian tank's machine gun plucked at their heels as they ran, hitting the tank's gunner. He fell face-first into the dirt in a spatter of bright red blood.

For a brief moment the terror and chaos of the sudden violent clash seemed to fade into an eerie smoke-filled silence. McGrath peered at his BMS. The interior of his tank was a haze of floating dust. Two more enemy tanks were several hundred yards further east, circling the battleground. He barked orders to his driver but suddenly Major Browne's voice cut across the comms unit, his voice like the fatal plunge of a knife, thick with despair and defeat. "More tanks emerging from the forest! At least another full company of T-72s advancing! Fallback, Red Four. Repeat. Fall back. All units… prepare to abandon the village!"

Chapter 10:

Wayland heard the Major's order, and his first reaction was a pang of proud soldier's defiance. He ordered his driver to reverse and take them east towards the looming Russian threat, then switched comms to the Platoon net.

"Red Four! Hold your position. I'm on my way. We're not retreating!"

"You want us to fight off an entire Company of Russians alone, One?" McGrath asked woefully.

"If we have to, yes!"

The Abrams dashed along the street that passed beneath the school building. A Russian tank was at the end of the road, just rounding a corner. Wayland could see dead bodies lying in the gutter.

"Designate tank! Load sabot!"

"Up!" the loader rammed a round into the breach and pirouetted out of the way of the wicked recoil.

"Identified!" J.J engaged the target.

"Fire and adjust!"

"On the way!"

The Abrams fired on the move, rocking on its tracks as the sabot round shot from the end of the long barrel. The tank drove through the smoke of the discharge and emerged to see the T-72 still sitting in the middle of the street. The enemy vehicle's turret was scarred and creased, but still functional.

"Re-engage!" Wayland snapped.

The loader thrust another round into the breach. "Up!"

"Identified!" J.J snarled. He thumbed the trigger and called, "On the way!" The enemy T-72 fired at the same instant. Both tanks disappeared behind grey smoke. The Russian tank's shot struck the front hull armor of Wayland's Abrams and left an ugly scar yet did not penetrate. But when the smoke cleared the Russian T-72 was in flames and burning like a desert oil fire.

"Target!" J.J confirmed.

The loader's voice cut across the instant of celebration. "We only have three rounds of sabot left."

"Then we have to make 'em count!" Wayland growled.

The driver swung the tank up onto the verge of the road and barged through a vegetable garden. The Abrams rocked and swayed across uneven ground. On his BMS Wayland could see Red Four about a hundred yards to his east. Ahead of McGrath's tank was a column of red enemy icons, beginning to emerge from the fringe of the forest.

"Red Four, I'm coming up on your left," Wayland spoke into the microphone attached to his CVC helmet. "Give me thirty seconds."

"We don't have that long, One!" McGrath's voice was strained. In the background Wayland could hear the muffled echo of men speaking to each other across the open line and then an instant later the sound of McGrath's tank firing crackled in his earpiece.

On the BMS he saw one of the red enemy icons fade then disappear from the screen. McGrath had killed one of the T-72s from a thousand yards.

Wayland ordered his tank to a sudden stop. He was partially concealed by a tree and a broken length of wooden fence. The tank see-sawed to a halt, rocking on its suspension. In his CITV he saw the enemy tanks. They were just emerging from the dark shadows of the forest, pouring through a cave-like opening between tall fir trees. One of the vehicles was on fire. Smoke and flaming sparks seemed to hang suspended in the air. The wheat field between the Americans and the Russians was dotted with smoking spot-fires. Wayland targeted the lead tank in the enemy column.

"Designate tank!"

"Up!"

A round landed close by. Wayland couldn't tell if it had been fired from one of the enemy tanks, or if the Russian howitzers had re-commenced their barrage. A cloud of flung dirt erupted in front of the Abrams and thudded across the turret. Wayland's ears sang with the deafening clamor of combat. The air inside the hull reeked of suffocating stale sweat and cordite.

"Identified!" J.J locked on to the enemy vehicle and engaged the tank's fire control system. The split-second delay seemed like an eternity.

"Fire!"

"On the way!"

The sabot round leaped from the barrel and the punch of recoil filled the stifling interior with dust. Across the wheat field the Russian tank suddenly vanished behind a violent flash of flame.

"Target!"

The next Russian tank in line swerved to avoid the wreckage and veered out into the open field. Its turret turned towards Wayland's tank and before the order to engage could be given, the enemy T-72's barrel bloomed in a flash of light and smoke. Wayland tensed instinctively, but the round missed by ten yards and tore through the kitchen of a nearby house.

"Red One! Red One! What the hell are you doing?" Major Browne's voice rasped across the Company net, sounding strident and stressed in his headset. "We are preparing to evacuate the village. Get the hell out of there!"

"We're buying you time, Command!"

For a crackling moment of static the radio fell utterly silent. When the Major responded at last, his voice sounded hollow, as if the words had been scrubbed of all emotion. "Confirm, Red One. Good luck. Out."

Wayland cut comms and grimly turned all his attention back to fighting. "Take that bastard out, J.J!"

His gunner locked on to the tank. "Identified!"

"Up!"

"Fire!"

But before J.J could squeeze the trigger the Russian tank suddenly exploded.

Wayland blinked and searched his BMS. He could see no other blue friendly icons displayed on the monitor. He peered right in confusion to where McGrath's tank was parked against a collapsed stone wall.

"What the fuck just happened?" J.J asked, bewildered.

Wayland shook his head. Then a second Russian tank erupted in flames, punched to a standstill by the impact of a sabot round. The T-72 disappeared behind a great tower of smoke and a few seconds later blew apart. The turret of the vehicle was blown upward by an internal explosion and flames leaped high into the sky.

"Jesus!"

"Red One! Hold your position! All units, hold your position!" Major Browne's voice was back on the Company net, this time almost light-headed with ecstatic relief. "The French have arrived!"

*

Three French Leclercs were positioned two thousand yards south of the village on a knoll of high ground that stood between Stare Lubiejewo and the town of Ostrow Mazowiecka. Three more French tanks were stationed to the west on a ridge sprinkled with trees. The six tanks were overwatch to cover the advance of the main column as it dashed along the road northwards.

The three Leclercs on the grassy knoll identified the second company of Russian T-72s as they emerged from the vast forest and engaged them at long range, killing two enemy vehicles as they broke from the dark shadows and into the wheat field. The three Leclercs west of the village engaged the Russian T-90s that were hull down behind the distant rise, covering the withdrawal of the BMP-3s from the farm fields.

Some analysts claimed the French-built MBT was the best tank in the world, pointing to its lighter weight and superb acceleration. Compared to the Abrams the Leclerc's titanium armor inserts and explosive-reactor armor bricks gave the vehicle superior side armor to the Abrams, and the tank also had a smaller turret profile, making it harder to hit. Regardless of opinion, the French tank was more than a match for the antiquated T-72s and could hold its own against the modern T-90.

Critics claimed the Leclerc was difficult to maintain, and pointed to the fact that, although it had been previously deployed on peacekeeping missions, it remained unbloodied in combat; no French Leclerc had ever fired a shot in battle. Now, for the first time, the steel beast would be put to the ultimate test.

Unlike most other contemporary tanks, the Leclerc had an auto-loader capable of loading twelve rounds per minute, and a three-man crew. Now that auto-loader feature proved its value as the surviving T-72s that emerged from the eastern forest sought to close on the village outskirts.

Two more of the Russian tanks were destroyed by the rapid-fire French Leclercs on overwatch and Wayland killed another with his last round of sabot. The remaining Russians turned north, not retreating into the forest but instead skirting along the edge of the woods, firing smoke to conceal their hasty withdrawal.

As the main French column approached the intersection, the Irish infantry grimly defending the outskirts gave a ragged cheer. Leclercs fanned east and west into the narrow streets. The first platoon of VBCI Armored Infantry Fighting Vehicles swerved into the school grounds and unloaded their cargo of troops. The infantry dashed forward, urgent and energetic, firing at the retreating enemy BMP-3s.

Major Brown threw down his binoculars and gasped a deep sigh of relief. He felt physically drained, made haggard by the unrelenting strain. He cuffed dusty grit from his eyes and added his voice to the cheers of his men.

*

"The enemy are vulnerable until they are organized," zampolit Alferov hissed, abandoning all pretense of deference to his Colonel's rank or authority. "We must hit them again immediately. They will not stand against a concerted attack!"

Colonel Pugacheva looked sickly and shaken. His skin appeared ashen grey, his eyes glassy and unfocussed. "Where is my air support?" he turned on the zampolit in a rage. "You promised me when the weather – "

"I promised you nothing!" Alferov snarled. The savagery in the political officer's face gave even the old Colonel pause. "You have all the troops and tanks you need. Attack the enemy immediately – or the next time I see you, Colonel, it will be as a witness at your State execution."

Pugacheva flinched as if he had been slapped in the face. A contemptuous snort of defiance crept to his lips but then slid away. He was afraid of the zampolit's sinister influence.

"Very well," the Colonel's shoulders slumped. He inhaled a deep breath, drew himself erect, and went walking towards his command vehicle.

*

They met briefly behind the school building, beneath a bullet-scarred tree from which every leaf had been stripped and most of the bark shredded in the fighting. Wayland was the last to appear, pausing first to arrange the transfer of White Four's remaining ammunition to his own Abrams.

When he arrived, Major Browne and a tall, immaculately uniformed Colonel of the French Armee De Terre were standing close together in quiet but urgent conversation. Major Browne made the introductions and Wayland shook hands with Colonel Jules Lefebvre. The French officer was a humorless, dour man with dark eyes and hollow cheeks. He bowed his head politely.

"Very glad to have you here, Colonel."

The Frenchman nodded. "But who knows for how long, eh? At the moment we are here, but the enemy is moving across a broad front and on several roads. Do not dig your trenches too deep. I fear our time in this hamlet is limited, yes?" his English was precise.

"We're here until we get fresh orders from Warsaw," Major Browne said tactfully.

"Oui, as are my troops, Major. But orders are as fickle as a pretty woman."

Beyond the tree, a French Captain stood like a traffic warden in the middle of the intersection, directing the VBCI's and several Leclerc tanks into the streets around the western outskirts. The rest of the French armor was being steered northeast, into the outlying buildings scattered around the village's football field from where they could cover the road north and the dense forest on their eastern flank. Lefebvre set up his command post in the parking lot of the hotel and kept six of the French MBTs in reserve. Wayland's five remaining tanks were withdrawn to the tree-covered ground on the opposite side of the road where the relieved remnants of the Irish Company were tending to their wounded.

Tank crewmen and infantry stood, numb and exhausted, like survivors of a terrible natural disaster. Some men exchanged cigarettes and MREs. Most simply sat or lay in the long grass staring blankly into space, their minds haunted by the nightmare of all they had endured. One young soldier wept softly and could not be consoled. Another man sat with his back against a tree, his knees drawn up, thumbing through a pocket Bible, his mouth moving fervently over the words.

Then the Russian howitzers suddenly opened fire again, and the world crashed back into hell.

*

The battle began as a brushfire of concealed movement behind the distant crest and then suddenly ignited when a Company of T-90 tanks supported by a dozen BMP-3s raced down the road from Lomza then veered into the farmhouse-littered fields east of the road. The enemy massed in a grove of woods two thousand yards north of the village, arranging themselves into a line of tanks with the troop carriers behind them.

When they burst into the open, they came across the undulating paddocks at high speed, dashing towards the line of hedgerows north of the football ground. The tanks charged past the ruined vehicles that had launched previous attacks and ran over the dead bodies of the infantry that had fallen.

To the Irish infantry resting behind the lines, the sound of the attack came as a distant muffle of engines and a fresh haze of smoke. They turned with a sense of foreboding and wondered what this new menace presaged. On the rooftop of the school building Major Browne turned his binoculars towards the sudden assault but could make out little of what was happening.

The French had two drones in the sky and Colonel Lefebvre watched the monitors from his command post. The French column was not equipped with the NATO Software Defined Radio system so communication between the Major and the Colonel was through a hand-held radio. Now, with the French assuming the responsibility for defending the village, Major Browne felt reduced to the role of an observer.

"Colonel," he keyed the radio. "Russian tanks and PC's attacking between the eastern edge of the road and the fringe of the forest. Company strength armor."

"Oui, Major," the French officer's voice was unruffled. "I have them in sight."

The Russian tanks opened fire as they advanced, but with no identified targets their first rounds merely added to the noise, chaos and destruction. A storage shed beside a farmhouse exploded, and a house closer to the village's outskirts burst into smoke and flames.

Then a column of T-72s erupted from the shadow of the woods, joining the T-90s on their flank, the two forces merging to form a crushing hammer blow. Belatedly, the Russian howitzers and field artillery behind the crest added their roar to the clamor, targeting the buildings near the eastern edge of the village. Soon the whole world seemed on fire.

Wayland appeared on the rooftop. He stood close to the Irish Major and watched the attack unfold. The French had six Leclerc tanks in hull-down positions forward of the east-west road that bisected the village. When the enemy tanks closed within one thousand yards, the French opened fire.

Two of the T-90s and a T-72 exploded in flames, killed instantly by French firepower. The rest of the Russian tanks continued their reckless charge, but now they had targets. They fired on the move. One sabot round struck a Leclerc low on the front hull, destroying the vehicle's right-side track and smashing a drive wheel, but the rest of the Russian fire flew wide of its marks. Behind the T-90s the BMP-3s stopped in a gentle fold of ground and disgorged their cargoes of infantry. A Company of Russian soldiers spilled from the vehicles and scattered into the long grass. Some skirted the verge of the Lomza road, working their way forward amongst the cover of the trees. The rest threw themselves down in the dirt and began to creep forward. Behind them the BMP-3s added the cough of their main guns to the clamor, firing 100mm HE-FRAG rounds into the closest buildings that might conceal French infantry or anti-tank teams.

Frenchmen began to die. A full company were spread east of the intersection, many in the bombed ruins of farm buildings, some in hastily dug shallow trenches. Five men were crushed to death when a HE-FRAG round collapsed the building they were concealed in. Two more died from enemy machine gun fire as the Russian infantry began to advance. The fighting flared and ebbed, then flared again as the leading Russian T-90s closed on the village outskirts.

The French infantry were armed with ERYX short-range portable anti-tank missile systems. The ERYX was a SACLOS-based (Semi-automatic command to line of sight) wire-guided system with a range of just six hundred meters. As the enemy tanks pressed forward, troops opened fire with the shoulder-mounted weapon. One operator died when he rose from behind a stone wall to launch at a T-90. He was cut down by the quick-reflexed Russian tank's gunner. A French Sergeant hidden in a toolshed lined up the enemy tank in his launcher's crosshairs and fired.

The missile ejected from the launch tube and the main sustainer motor ignited. The ERYX was a wire-guided anti-tank missile, steered by two vanes. It took almost three seconds to reach the tank in which time the Sergeant had to remain fearlessly still, continually pointing the sighting device at the target until the missile struck. Bullets tore chunks of wood from the building around him. Dust and dirt kicked up into his face. He gritted his teeth, held his position, and then flung himself down, gasping, the instant the missile detonated.

The tandem-charged HEAT warhead slammed into the Russian T-90's turret and the vehicle erupted in a whoosh of fire. The earth shook from the ferocity of the explosion and the tank stopped dead on its tracks. Two more ERYX missiles accounted for T-72s and the Leclercs killed three more T-90s without sustaining damage.

In an instant the momentum of the battle turned. The Russians recoiled – and the French tanks impulsively attacked.

Wayland watched in awe and incredulity. The enemy armor had been defeated. They had reached the hedgerow and once again been halted. Now they milled in confusion while behind them the BMP-3s began to fall back. Only the Russian infantry held their ground, still firing and moving as they edged closer to the village.

"What the fuck are they doing?" Wayland stared in disbelief.

The five serviceable Leclercs burst from their hull-down positions in great billows of blue exhaust, shaking off dust as they emerged into open ground. They made a brave, bold sight, machine guns spitting flame.

They advanced in loose formation, suddenly accelerating and switching to their main guns as they closed on the enemy. The Russian tankers were caught unprepared. They began to fall back, firing as they withdrew.

Like cavalry of old, the Leclercs spurred into the final charge, dashing directly for the enemy. One of the T-90s paused long enough from its retreat to fire a snap-shot at the closest French vehicle. The round clanged off the tank's front armor. The Russian fired again, this time while reversing. The round missed the French tank completely. Then the French were amongst the Russians in open ground and at close range. Two T-72s were brutally blown apart and left smoldering wrecks. Another T-90 had its turret ripped off as it erupted in flames.

The few remaining enemy tanks retreated in confusion across the field occupied by their infantry and BMP-3s. The Russians lost all order and the battlefield became a bloody slaughterhouse. Two of the APCs collided in their haste to flee. Several Russian soldiers were crushed in the milling chaos. The Leclercs waded through the mayhem and there were too many targets to massacre them all. A dozen Russian infantry were gunned down by machine gun fire. They died screaming, but the sounds of their deaths were drowned out by the crash of sabot rounds and the whine of straining engines. Some Russian infantry threw their arms up in surrender. A BMP-3 driver tried to steer for the safety of the road, but a HEAT shell from a Leclerc disintegrated the vehicle.

Wayland watched in awe from the rooftop and saw the entire Russian attack chewed to pieces. The Leclercs were rampaging amongst the enemy, slaughtering and killing, turning and firing, sprinting and swerving until the ground was drenched in blood and littered with smoldering steel fragments beneath a cloud of black oily smoke.

A Russian company of T-90s and a Company of T-72s had been destroyed. A dozen APCs and almost a hundred Russian infantry had been torn to fragments. But still the French thirst for blood could not be slaked. The charge had filled the paddocks with death but the Frenchmen were drunk on their success and frenzied for the fight. The Leclercs formed up in disarray and raced towards the Lomza road in pursuit of glory.

"What are they doing?" Wayland gaped, momentarily sicked with foreboding. "They can't attack the whole fucking Russian Army!"

Major Browne snatched for his radio. "Colonel! Call your tanks back! They're charging to their deaths!"

The lead Leclerc reached the verge of the road north and suddenly exploded, blown apart by a Russian RPG fired from close range. The second Leclerc was struck broadside by a sabot round fired from a T-90 on the skyline. The remaining three Leclercs suddenly stalled in confusion and then began to edge back towards the hedgerow.

"Oh, Christ," Wayland groaned. He felt physically ill. The third Leclerc in the group shuddered and then was consumed by a fireball of bright orange flame. The turret hatch opened and a crewman crawled into the light. He was bleeding badly. He flung himself down into the long grass and began to crawl towards the village. A shredding breeze thinned the veil of battlefield smoke for a moment and beyond it emerged more Russian infantry. A burst of automatic fire rang out and the French tanker slumped to the ground dead.

The surviving two Leclercs reversed towards the safety of the village. They swerved, erratic with panic, trying to throw off the enemy's aim, firing their machine guns wildly and ejecting smoke cannisters to conceal their humiliating flight.

Wayland continued to watch on, appalled. "The stupid bastards," he muttered. "The stupid ill-disciplined bastards…"

A T-72 concealed in the fringes of the great forest destroyed the fourth Leclerc by striking the tank's right-side track, mangling three of the roadwheels and hobbling the steel beast in the middle of the mud-churned football field. The crew bailed out and scrambled for cover. They never made it. All three men were cut down by Russian machine gun fire. Two men cried out as bullets smashed into their backs. The Leclerc's commander was hit in the thigh and fell face-first into the mud. He lay still for a moment and then staggered gamely to his feet. An enemy sniper put a bullet through the back of his head.

Wayland's shoulders slumped. His face turned ashen with the obscenity of what he had witnessed.

Rain started to fall, and with it came a fresh barrage of Russian howitzer shells.

West of the road, the enemy launched another assault.

*

The second wave of the Russian attack rose from the dead ground behind the rise and appeared on the skyline as a wall of charging tanks and APCs.

It was war in the classic Russian way; the massed assault supported by artillery which was designed to punch a hole through the heart of the enemy for fast-moving infantry carriers to pour through.

The Russians had tried this tactic across these fields once before and failed, so this time, to ensure certain victory, more armor and more APCs had been flung forward until the ground trembled and the roar of revving engines was a noise so loud as to numb the senses.

The steel battering ram came rumbling across the farm fields. Ahead of them artillery shells fell in a rolling barrage, advancing in front of the attack, filling the air with smoke and explosions.

Wayland and Major Browne watched from the rooftop with growing anxiety. The eight French Leclercs protecting the village's western flank opened fire, and the Russians began to take punishment. Two T-90s lost their tracks and stalled, forcing the following vehicles to swerve around them.

The smoke thickened until nothing could be seen. The Russian artillery switched the focus of their fire onto the fringes of the village. The crash of explosions became unrelenting. Frenchmen in their trenches began to die in ones and twos. The trickle of injured and dead turned into a steady stream. The bombardment unleashed by the Russians was horrific. Shell fragments filled the air with death. One French Corporal had his throat cut by flying debris and died choking on his own blood. A young Private lost two fingers of his left hand and squealed in pain until a Sergeant bellowed at him angrily to shut up.

And still the Russian tidal wave of armor advanced. A Leclerc near the western fringe of the village fired through the smoke at a T-90 and missed, only to strike the hull of trailing BMP-3, obliterating the vehicle and slaughtering the men inside. Another French tank scored a kill on a T-90 from a thousand yards. The sabot round punched through the Russian vehicle's hull armor and blew the tank into fragments. Three more T-90s were destroyed by French fire before the Russians reached the hedgerows outside the village. The BMP-3s unloaded their infantry and the men swarmed forward through the swirling smoke, firing from the hip as they charged.

The French infantry fired back. Machine guns posted along the street cut a swathe through the advancing enemy but still they pressed forward. The American mortar carrier opened fire, lobbing rounds into the blood-churned fields. Men screamed and died, officers shouted orders, and automatic fire slashed holes through the smoke until the battlefield became a confused turmoil of dark shapes and death.

The first Russians reached the outlying village buildings and the infantry battle turned into a vicious street fight. Around them the two tank forces exchanged punches from close range. A Leclerc was destroyed by a Russian RPG rocket and burst into flames. A T-90 emerged through a wall of smoke and was blindsided by a French shoulder-fired ERYX missile.

The Russian artillery fire stopped, and in its place the noise of the ground battle rose to a crescendo. A BMP-3 disappeared within a column of black boiling smoke. Men inside the burning vehicle spilled out through the back doors into the mud-churned grass and were cut down by a machine gun.

The French infantry began to edge backwards. The Russians pressed forward. The French surrendered the outlying buildings and retreated across the narrow street. Grenades exploded, and the fighting broke down into bitter squad-level skirmishes amongst the rubble and ruins.

A downpour of rain and a sudden gust of chill wind tore the curtain of smoke apart and revealed the horror of the fight.

Wayland stared in abject despair. The French infantry were pinned down by unrelenting Russian fire and soon the Leclercs would be in danger of being surrounded.

"We've lost the outskirt buildings," Wayland said tensely. "The Russians are into the first row of houses, and they're pushing hard. In ten minutes, the entire west flank of our defense is going to collapse."

Major Browne studied the scene for a brief moment and smiled a thin humorless challenge. "Then you have ten minutes left to do something about it, Lieutenant."

Wayland turned on his heel and sprinted for the stairwell. "Tell the Colonel I'm coming," he shouted as he ran. "And tell him I want his six reserve Leclercs."

*

From the elevated vantage point of the school building's rooftop, the shape of the battle had been apparent to Wayland. The French infantry were swinging back, like a gate, from the hinge point of the intersection. The troops on the western outskirts, hardest hit by the impact of the Russian battering ram, were in disarray. Closer to the intersection, the French were clinging to their positions, but if the gate was forced open completely the Leclercs would be marooned without the ground support they needed to keep Russian anti-tank teams at arm's length. Once the Russians overwhelmed the flank, their BMP-3s would dash around behind the allied positions and roll through the village, slaughtering and destroying. Wayland knew what he had to do; somehow he had to force the 'gate' closed again by reinforcing the western edge of the village and pushing the Russians back.

Down at ground level, as Wayland ran towards the motel, the battlefield was a place of dust and smoke and explosions. Machine guns rattled incessantly, punctuated by the thundering boom of tanks firing. The 'crump!' of grenades sounded shallow in comparison. More buildings were on fire. Others, already burned to the ground, still smoldered. The blacktop was strewn with rubble and flung clods of earth, ripped from the ground by howitzer shells.

Wayland reached his tank and shouted at the men to mount up. The Abrams crews scrambled into their tanks. Colonel Lefebvre appeared from inside his command vehicle trailed by several junior officers. He looked bleak with apprehension.

"My Leclerc commanders have orders to follow you. Here," he handed Wayland a radio. "It is the only way you will be able to communicate."

Wayland kept his instructions to the six French tankers simple. "We're going to reinforce the western flank. Our infantry there are being pushed back by overwhelming numbers. I want to hit the enemy hard and force them to retreat into the fields. Don't engage Russian armor – leave that to the tanks already defending the position. It's the infantry we want to crush. Understand?"

Heads nodded, then everyone scattered as if a live hand grenade had been thrown into their midst. Men clambered aboard their tanks, engines snarled to life. Wayland saw Sergeant McGrath standing upright in his tank's turret. He gave the Sergeant a thumbs-up and a jaunty, confident smile. The Sergeant saluted him and then dropped down out of sight, pulling his turret hatch shut.

Wayland led the rag-tag column of tanks due west along a narrow back street that ran parallel to the fighting. When he reached the last house on the block, he ordered his driver to turn and told J.J to switch his weapon selector to coax.

Both the tank's machine guns carried full ammunition loads. Wayland could hear fighting through the thick armor of his hull, so loud that he wanted to cringe from it, but dared not.

"Forward!"

The five battle-scarred, fire-scorched Abrams' lead the attack. The Leclercs followed but did not maintain formation.

Instead they bludgeoned their own path through the gardens and fences so that all eleven MBTs crashed into the open at the same moment.

The tanks emerged through the swirling smoke like monsters from a nightmare and slammed into the Russian flank, machine guns blazing. Wayland manned the tank's CROWS system and fired the Abrams' 50cal from within the turret while JJ operated the coax. Between them the savage hail of bullets took a gruesome toll.

A Russian platoon was scattered across three houses, firing from the ruins at a handful of French infantry on the far side of the road. The 50cal tore the enemy's hiding places to pieces, punching through wooden walls, tearing chunks out of concrete, slashing and shredding everything within sight. Spent shell casings spewed from the weapon and fell like rain. The Russians ceased firing and cowered in the ruins while the buildings were demolished around them. A dozen enemy soldiers died in the brief fury. Others fled the maelstrom. JJ hunted them down with the coax.

Sergeant McGrath's Abrams jounced onto the street through a cloud of dust and churned earth. A Russian infantry squad were firing at the French from behind a waist-high stone wall. McGrath's gunner sprayed the position with coax fire.

"Save your ammunition!" McGrath snarled. He ordered his driver to advance. The tank mounted the gutter and charged through the stone barricade, crushing three of the Russians it had concealed. The rest of the squad scattered in confusion.

"Now kill the bastards!" McGrath grunted. The gunner went to work and the coax sprayed chattering death.

All along the line the American and French tanks blazed at the enemy until, squad by squad, the Russians were killed or forced back. In their wake, the French infantry came forward courageously and reclaimed the outskirts of the village. For a tense moment the battle hung in the balance. Wayland had closed the swinging gate, but his hold on the flank was tenuous. Now the enemy tanks and APCs must be beaten back.

The Abrams' switched to their main guns and began picking off enemy BMPs. Within sixty seconds seven troop carriers were burning hulks.

The Russian tanks began to edge back and the surviving BMP-3s followed. From beyond the rise a fresh barrage of artillery shells began to rain down on the village, firing smoke to cover the ragged withdrawal.

Wayland knew the fight had been won, but it had been a desperately near-run thing. He punched open the turret hatch and let cool air flood the interior.

When the column of tanks returned to the motel parking lot, Wayland saw Major Browne and Colonel Lefebvre waiting for him. He climbed down from the Abrams. The French officer shook his hand.

"Bold and brave, Lieutenant. I commend you."

Wayland was quick to deflect the praise. "We couldn't have done it without your tanks, Colonel. Please pass on my thanks to your crews."

Major Browne clapped Wayland on the shoulder and was about to speak when the sight of a running soldier distracted him.

"Sir," a French Lieutenant interrupted with a crisp salute. "Warsaw Operations Control is on the line."

Colonel Lefebvre excused himself with a courteous nod and turned for his command vehicle. The APC was a Renault four-wheeled VAB. The armored double-doors at the rear of the vehicle were open revealing a windowless interior with an inward-facing bench and a small map table against one wall. The other side of the vehicle was crammed with radio equipment and three NCO operators. Lefebvre strode up a short ramp and sat down on the end of the bench. One of the operators handed him a headset.

The exchange took several minutes. Neither Wayland or Major Browne spoke French, but they could tell by the frown on the Colonel's face and the rising frustration in his voice that he was disputing his orders. Finally Lefebvre gave a Gallic shrug of bitter exasperation and snatched at the headset. He came back down the ramp, his features grave.

"My tanks and APCs have been ordered to withdraw five kilometers to the town of Ostrow Mazowiecka," the French Colonel explained. "Major, your infantry – and your tanks, Lieutenant – are relieved. Your units are to return to Warsaw with great honor," he stiffened and saluted respectfully.

"You're falling back?" Wayland asked in dismay.

"Yes," Lefebvre's expression reflected his disappointment. "The entire Russian Army is in front of us. Warsaw Command wants my unit to fall back on the road from Zambrow to prevent an enemy outflanking maneuver. If we don't withdraw immediately we are in danger of being encircled and cut off by a Russian armored column closing fast from the southeast."

"When?" Major Browne asked.

"I have been ordered to disengage the enemy immediately."

"Christ on his cross!"

"Gentlemen, I can delay my evacuation for thirty minutes, but no more than that. You need to withdraw your tanks and troops. You don't have a single minute to spare. Once the Russians sense I am falling back, they will attack and seize the village."

Chapter 11:

The remaining Abrams were formed up in column on the shoulder of the road opposite the motel. The valiant remnants of the Irish Guards were mounted onto the back of the battle-scarred vehicles. The men's faces were haggard, their eyes dulled by the horror they had faced and endured. Major Browne and Wayland stood at the intersection and stared north.

"We gave the Ruskies one hell of a fight, so we did," the Irishman looked impossibly tired. His face was drawn, and powdered with sweat-stained grime.

"There's still the IED," Wayland said gamely. "We could give them one final bloody nose they would never forget…"

The air overhead filled with a sudden shrieking whistle and a second later a Russian howitzer shell landed in the village, striking the corner of the abandoned school building. A heartbeat later another shell struck the western outskirts of the bomb-ruined settlement.

Major Browne smiled thinly and raised his voice above the clamor of the explosions. "It's a suicide option," he cautioned. "Someone would have to stay behind to detonate the device."

"I'll do it."

The Irish Major met Wayland's steady, determined gaze. He saw Sergeant McGrath sprinting along the road towards them. The American Sergeant was shouting urgently as he ran. "We've got to move out now!"

The Major ignored McGrath's warning. His expression turned suddenly roguish. "Toss you for it."

Before Wayland could protest the Major fished a coin from the bottom of his pocket and grinned. His eyes flashed with a devilish buccaneer's bravado.

"Tails," said Wayland as another howitzer shell landed north of the intersection, flattening two trees and gouging a crater from the earth.

Major Browne spun the coin into the air and let it hit the ground. Wayland stooped to examine it. "It's a tail," he said. "I'll stay and – "

Behind him, Major Browne pulled his sidearm from its holster. "You've done more than enough, Lieutenant," he said softly. "It's my job to do." He tapped Wayland above the ear with the butt of the weapon.

Wayland collapsed unconscious to the ground just as Sergeant McGrath reached them. "Get your Lieutenant out of here, Sergeant. And when he wakes up..," the Irish officer thought for a second, "...tell him it was my honor to serve with him."

*

Colonel Pugacheva stood on the crest of the gentle rise, flanked by zampolit Alferov and his aides, and stared at the low smoking ruins of Stare Lubiejewo through his binoculars. He saw a bustle of movement on the streets. He peered more closely through the scrims of drifting smoke and realized with a sudden leap of giddy relief that the enemy were retreating. The French tanks which had arrived just in time to thwart his last assault were falling back along the road south of the village.

Pugacheva swung the binoculars left and right. The French APCs too, were withdrawing. He saw soldiers scrambling into the back of the troop carriers as they prepared to evacuate the settlement. The Russian Colonel threw down his binoculars, turned, and beckoned to his senior aide.

"We have won the village! The French are falling back! Release the tanks immediately!"

*

Major Browne turned on his heel and dashed for the rubble of the school building, from where he could sight the intersection and time the moment he detonated the IED. The air was filled with the whistling whine of inbound howitzer shells; one exploded in dead ground to the east of the village and three more fell around the hotel. The 'crump!' of each blast shook the earth. Dirt and smoke swirled in the air. Then the shelling stopped abruptly and the sound of approaching tanks carried on the fragile stillness.

The T-90s came dashing down the road in column formation. The lead vehicle was firing its machine gun. Short angry bursts of bullets smashed into the ruined houses close to the intersection, tearing fragments from the debris. Major Browne ducked behind a brick wall and stared diagonally across the street to where the first tank would emerge from behind a clump of blackened tree stumps.

The sound of the Russian tanks reached a snarling whine. The Major could feel his heart pounding against the cage of his ribs. He pulled the radio from his belt and clutched it tightly between bleeding dirty hands.

Then the wicked 'crack!' of a high-powered rifle plucked at the air just an inch past his left ear, the bullet's path so close that he felt the searing heat of its passage against his cheek. He flinched instinctively and started wild-eyed to the north through a crack in the mortar.

"Christ on his cross!" he muttered. There was a Russian sniper somewhere in the houses on the outskirts of the village. Major Browne scrambled ten yards to his left. He could hear the enemy tanks clearly now. He heard the squeaking clatter of their steel tracks and the relentless chatter of their machine guns. They were spraying bursts of suppressing fire as they approached the intersection. He heard the first Russian tank rattle past, and then the second vehicle in the column followed.

Major Browne closed his eyes, drew two deep breaths, and pounced to his feet, leaving himself exposed. He stared at the intersection. The third T-90 in the column was almost at the crossing. His dry cracked lips moved. "God, please look after my wife and the wee ones…" and then triggered the IED.

For a heartbeat nothing happened.

Then everything happened at once.

The ground around the intersection erupted upward in a seismic, volcanic explosion of earth, flying chunks of blacktop, and gravel. The tank at the crossing was heaved off its track by the violence of the brutal eruption and hurled onto its side. The vehicle skidded to a steel-screaming halt in a vast detonation of roaring fire and smoke. The overturned tank slewed across the middle of the road. The track unraveled and shredded into pieces of flung shrapnel. A leaping fireball engulfed the T-90 and then the sky filled with a dark oily billow of cloud. Men screamed in pain and shock. The tankers inside the vehicle hammered their fists feebly against the hatches but could not escape. They burned to death inside the steel coffin.

Major Browne's craggy face split into a grin of triumph. His whole attention was fixed on the chaos the explosion had caused, so that he did not see the enemy sniper take vengeful aim.

He did not hear the wicked retort of the bullet, for the impact of it struck him full in the chest before the crack of the shot could carry on the air. There was just the sudden hammer-blow punch of the bullet striking, and then the dismay and the bewildered shock as he was flung to the ground.

He lay in the ruins of the school building, and groped with his hand to feel for the wound. His trembling fingers crawled down across his chest and then turned bright red with warm sticky blood. The pain came then; a terrible burning agony so that he felt his whole body was aflame. He screwed his eyes shut and sobbed for fresh breath. He felt himself begin to shake and then his lower body turned numb. He thought about his wife and his children. An image of them playing happily at the seaside bloomed in his mind, so bright, so perfect, that he could almost smell the sea salt and hear the laughter of the wee ones.

He opened his eyes one final time and saw the sun bright in the sky overhead between drifting scrims of black smoke. He tried to smile, but his lips seemed frozen. He gave a last wheeze of breath and went eternally still.

*

Wayland came groggily to wakefulness by the side of the road three kilometers south of the village. He was propped upright against the trunk of a tree, sitting in long grass. Sergeant McGrath's huge hulking shape loomed over him.

Wayland blinked and swayed. Then a huge explosion split the air and a vast column of smoke rose into the sky somewhere to the north beyond the bend in the road.

Wayland looked over his shoulder and realization struck him. He tried to scramble to his feet but Sergeant McGrath pinned him down with ease.

"It was the Major's choice," McGrath said gently. "Now it's done. It's over."

"Oh, the bastard!" Wayland groaned.

"Maybe. But he was our kind of bastard, and a hero. He said it was an honor to serve with you. He wanted you to know."

Wayland got to his feet and stared at the rising cloud of black smoke for a long time. He found with no surprise that his eyes were shiny with tears.

Facebook: https://www.facebook.com/NickRyanWW3
Website: https://www.worldwar3timeline.com

Acknowledgements:

The greatest thrill of writing, for me, is the opportunity to research the subject matter and to work with military, political and historical experts from around the world. I had a lot of help researching this book from the following people. I am forever grateful for their willing enthusiasm and cooperation. Any remaining technical errors are mine.

Dion Walker Sr.

Sergeant First Class (Retired) Dion Walker Sr, served 21 proud years in the US Army with deployments during Operation Desert Shield/Storm, Operation Intrinsic Action and Operation Iraqi Freedom. For 17 years he was a tanker in several Armor Battalions and Cavalry Squadrons before spending 4 years as an MGS (Stryker Mobile Gun System) Platoon Sergeant in a Stryker Infantry company.

More than anyone else, Dion's advice and knowledge made this novel possible and I am forever in his debt for his enthusiastic support, his prompt help with research questions, and his willingness to ensure that each scene was as authentic as possible.

Jill Blasy:

Jill has the editorial eye of an eagle! I trust Jill to read every manuscript, picking up typographical errors, missing commas, and for her general 'sense' of the book. Jill has been a great friend and a valuable part of my team for several years.

Jan Wade:

Jan is my Personal Assistant and an indispensable part of my team. She is a thoughtful, thorough, professional and persistent pleasure to work with. Chances are, if you're reading this book, it's due to Jan's engaging marketing and promotional efforts.

Nicholas Moran 'The Chieftain':

US Army National Guard officer and tank historian, Nicholas Moran, is the in-house historian for the gaming company responsible for 'World of Tanks', and has a Youtube channel with over 180,000 subscribers. He is an acknowledged tank expert who contributed greatly to my understanding of how tank battles are fought, battlefield management systems, and a whole host of other technical details that ultimately added to the novel's authenticity.

You can find out about Nicholas here:

https://www.youtube.com/user/TheChieftainWoT

Printed in Great Britain
by Amazon